Pride Publishing books

Someday I[illegible]
An Immoveal[illegible]

The Borders War
One Breath, One Bullet
Dominant Predator
Powerless
Falling, One by One
Strength of the Rising Sun

Anthologies
Semper Fidelis: Anomaly

The Borders War

DOMINANT PREDATOR

S.A. MCAULEY

Dominant Predator
ISBN # 978-1-78651-851-4

Interior text design by Claire Siemaszkiewicz
Pride Publishing

Published in 2016 by Pride Publishing, Newland House, The Point, Weaver Road, Lincoln, LN6 3QN, United Kingdom.

Pride Publishing is a subsidiary of Totally Entwined Group Limited.

DOMINANT PREDATOR

Dedication

To the guy who owns that pickup truck in the Meijer parking lot.

Chapter One

August 2558
Merq Grayson's 34th year
The Continental States

Pain. Blinding, searing, blood-vaporizing pain.

No matter how many times I went through a transport, the effect was always the same. Debilitating.

My body seized up, spasmed, and I felt the moment my particles scattered. A vast emptiness fell upon me, one that I'd come to associate with agony, even though that exact moment was the most peaceful of the transition.

But what came next caught me unaware. Every. Single. Time.

The world—my existence—flashed out of being then slammed back. A coalescing of atoms and cells, blood thrumming, heart pumping. I sucked in a desperate breath that burned, my lungs fighting the sudden inhalation. I reached out for something—someone?—gritted my teeth and found my awareness. Remembered.

My shot. The premiere. The bunker.

Armise.

"Fuck," a labored voice behind me groaned. An arm gripped me tighter, drawing my twitching body into an iron embrace.

Too close. Too much. This—this intimacy—wasn't what happened after a kill.

I let my head fall to the cool, smooth floor and tried to calm my racing heartbeat and spasming muscles as I yanked the hand off my stomach.

Armise let go of me without protest. I rolled away from him then to my feet, hesitating for only a fraction of a second as I stood. The nerves in my legs tingled. A rush of that potent drug surge thrummed through my veins—only remnants now, but enough to dull the pain of transport.

"Great shot." A woman's voice came from the other side of the room.

I shielded my eyes from the glare of the white ceramic floor and took in the petite frame of the woman leaning against the wall, her black skin in sharp contrast to the sterile silver metal walls.

I grunted in response to Jegs and looked down at Armise.

He was on his back on the transport floor, eyes closed, the sinew of his neck and veins popping out with the effort it was taking for him to get the pain under control.

"I thought you only traveled via transport," I said with disbelief and just a hint of a taunt.

Armise's eyes snapped open, caught me in a clear, challenging glare. "Your transport technology is obviously inferior to Singapore's. No wonder you rarely travel this way. How do we know that each time we transport it's not slowly killing us?"

"We don't," Jegs answered for me as she tipped her head in Armise's direction. "So. You're a traitor."

Armise sat up, threw an arm over his knees and scratched at his beard. "I suppose so," he answered without flinching. "I am guessing from the slashes that you are Jegs. You weren't exactly conscious the first time we met."

Jegs narrowed her eyes and didn't answer him. From the brief blankness that overtook her eyes, I guessed she was trying to access the memory of her captivity in Singapore. Trying to decide if Armise was the one who'd nearly killed her.

"He wasn't the one who tortured you in Singapore," I reassured her.

She didn't take her focus off Armise. "You sure about that?"

I shrugged. "Relatively. Where's the president?"

She pushed off the wall and started to the door. "Should be here. He was set to transport in with the newly promoted General Neveed Niaz right after your shot. Simion is on that detail."

"Just how many transport rooms do you have?" Armise asked as he stood.

"Enough—"

"Four—"

Jegs and I answered at the same time.

I pointed at her. "This ends here."

She gave a clipped nod, restrained anger evident in her pursed lips and the flat black of her eyes.

"Order received." She approached me and held out her hand, two capsules of surge resting on her palm. "For the external damage this one did to you in the tunnels."

I took the capsules, downed one and threw the other to Armise. Immediately I felt the press of my swollen left eye easing and my injured shoulder loosening.

Above our heads a high-pitched whine gained in volume, followed closely by a screeching explosion and the muted patter of debris drumming to the ground feet above us on the surface streets of the capital. The ground beneath my feet shook, dirt scattering from the packed earth ceiling.

"What's that sound?" I said, my voice breaking from my inability to draw in a full breath.

Jegs cocked her head as if she wasn't sure what I was referring to, even as the room continued to reverberate around us. Another thundering boom came from above and the transport platform shook.

She pointed up, a wicked grin exposing her teeth. "Those, Colonel, are artillery shells. Welcome to the Revolution."

* * * *

It was unnerving, to say the least.

I had been prepared for war of this type—messy, bloody, loud and more unpredictable than anything I'd ever experienced—but nothing could have prepared me for the unending movement. I felt each burst of gunfire. Each drop of a bomb. Each *crackle-snap-flash* of grenades. We were underground, but the ground moved as if it were water instead of the steadiness of bedrock.

The president's bunker in the capital was our headquarters for now. Meant to be used for days, not weeks, and certainly not permanently, as we coordinated the initial push against Opposition forces. The president had been adamant about the temporary nature of our stay. If his people were out on the streets fighting, then he wouldn't be hidden underground.

This station would serve to coordinate troops, but the president wouldn't be staying here and neither would his second-in-command General Neveed Niaz, my handler up until minutes ago, when I'd finally completed the mission I'd been training for most of my life—to kill the Premiere of Singapore. I'd assassinated him with the first bullet to be shot in public in over two hundred years. That bullet was the first to find its mark in this war, but it would be far from the last.

Up until the moment my shot split his head open, the premiere had been the leader of the Opposition, a faction set on maintaining power with the most elite of society. Before the Borders War had started three hundred years ago the population of the world had skyrocketed to unsustainable numbers in the billions. Rampant disease propelled by food shortages and contaminated water had started the purge, but the war had been the final fatal action.

While the war had brought the world population down to the hundreds of millions, strife had dropped that number even further, widening the gap between those who had everything and those who had nothing.

The Revolution hoped to turn that tide.

That I had managed to remain hidden as a double operative—supposedly on the payroll of the Opposition, yet loyal to the Revolution—for more than a decade was a miracle unto itself.

And that Armise Darcan had turned traitor to Singapore so he could make sure I made it out of that stadium alive after my shot was something I hadn't had time to fully consider yet.

Armise was at my side as we exited the transport room, his demeanor steely calm once again after the brutal transport from the stadium. He wore his silver and cobalt blue People's Republic of Singapore uniform and his silver-streaked hair was mussed. He slicked the errant strands back. He didn't make eye contact with me as we walked down the hallway, choosing instead to meet each wondering stare that passed over us. His uniform proclaimed his status as a Singaporean, but that he wasn't under guard or bound like a prisoner raised more than a few curious glances. His unchallenged presence in what was likely the safest place anywhere in the States brought more attention to us than I was used to.

It didn't help that his face had been broadcast across the globe next to mine as the world prepared for the Olympics. The people here recognized him—but only as an enemy to the States and possibly to the Revolution. We were a paranoid group at best. Careful was a more diplomatic word, but still hyped up from the shot and uneasy from the continuous roll of the floor underneath me, I wasn't feeling very diplomatic at the moment.

We approached the president's transport room—Armise at my right shoulder and Jegs trailing him.

The doors to the room swished open as we approached and the president emerged first.

He turned in my direction, a triumphant smile on his face. "Good shot."

"So I've heard."

The president bowed deeply to Armise but didn't say anything else as he proceeded down the hallway toward the control room.

The rest of his entourage gave Armise a wide berth, choosing to ignore his presence or blatantly sneer at him. I wondered how many of them knew about Armise besides what intel and rumors had told them.

'Traitor,' Jegs had called him.

I wondered what they would think of me if they knew I was fucking him. And that I had been for almost a third of my life now.

Simion—a fellow Peacemaker, and a man who'd been under my command for the last thirteen years—took wide steps to catch up to my side. He laid a hand on my left shoulder. "I believed you'd turned rogue. I should have known."

I eyed him, not bothering to hide my disdain. "You should have."

He stepped back, physically shrinking from my reply. Good.

In front of me, Neveed walked next to the president, talking to him in hushed tones. He must have felt me looking at him, because he turned and gave me a nod of acknowledgment.

I tipped my chin at him in response. That movement was the only recognition I would get from Neveed that I'd done my job. He beckoned me forward and stepped out of the way so I could walk with the president.

"So what's next?" I asked the president.

He smiled at me. "That's the first time you've ever asked me that question."

"I didn't expect to be asking it."

He tipped his head toward Armise, who kept steadfastly to my right shoulder. "It was better that way."

"Okay," I replied without question.

He studied me as if he didn't believe that it would be that easy, then nodded in response. "Okay then. Come meet the rest of the Revolution command."

"It's not my place."

"It is now. You are the most recognizable face on the planet." He pushed into the double metal doors of the bunker's command center and pointed at the screen at the front of the room. I stopped in my tracks.

Unlike the normal biocomp 5 screens—BC5 for short—that appeared at the flick of a wrist when the wearer had a comm chip, this screen filled the entire back wall. The room was controlled chaos, but everyone came to a complete stop when we entered, assessing eyes flitting nervously between Armise and me. The president didn't appear fazed as he maneuvered around their frozen forms.

The image of me with the Winchester shouldered—my finger hovering over the trigger, cheek just off the barrel, brown eye focused through the scope—stared back at me, as if the camera had been placed directly in front of my shot. There must have been a camera located somewhere on the dais where I couldn't spot it. My finger tightened on the trigger and the gun exploded, smoke rising from the barrel and a gold bullet exiting in slow motion.

The press didn't have any compunction about broadcasting the moment of impact. Also in painful, crystal-clear slow motion. The premiere didn't have a chance to react. The bullet entered his forehead at direct center—between his eyes, at the point of his third eye, Neveed had once taught me. His head split apart obscenely at this speed of replay. Bone shattering, blood droplets flying into the air—splattering, running down the silver metal of the throne—the back of his head opening to the elements as he slammed back, slumped forward, then off the chair.

Then the news footage came back to a shot of me. Armise's arms around my waist and us disappearing in a zap of electrically charged matter dispersal.

Behind me Armise cleared his throat.

I pointed to the screen. "That's counterproductive to my job."

The president watched the footage as it repeated—the same ten-second loop—over and over again as he spoke to me. "Your job is the Revolution. You are the face of our movement now, Merq." He gestured with a hand over his shoulder. "Update me, Neveed."

With that I knew he was done with me. At least for now.

"It really was a good shot," Armise said when I tracked back to him.

"You're surprised?"

The corner of Armise's lips tipped up in a restrained smile. He crossed his arms as he leaned against the wall. "Nearly perfect."

I didn't let it show that his attempt did cut at me a bit. He was a better sniper than I was. It was a fact that both of us were aware of. But that shot couldn't have been more perfect and both of us knew that.

I crossed my arms and stubbornly matched his stance.

Heads continued to turn in our direction as movement and discussion restarted in the room. The expression in most of their eyes and on their faces was one of trepidation. Possibly fear. Maybe respect or awe. It was difficult to ascertain. They were all wary for sure.

I could understand why. Armise and I were the two biggest men in the room by far. Standing shoulder to shoulder, even in this at-ease position, we took up almost the entire back wall of the packed control room.

And all the evidence they needed of our deadliness and competence in that area was on an endless loop in front of them. If they hadn't known who we were by reputation then there was no longer doubt.

The realization made me stand straighter, pull my shoulders back and clench my jaw as I took a deep inhalation through my nose.

Before this no one had been aware of just how dangerous I was until they had to fight me face-to-face or at the end of my rifle. Anyone who had hadn't lived to report on my skill. Only Armise had faced me in that scenario and survived. But now there was no question as to my power.

I'd never felt more indestructible.

Neveed began debriefing the president. "Fighting is heaviest in the capital due to the influx of Opposition followers for the games. Unfortunately, it's just as heavy in the DCR." He swiped a hand across a desk and changed the single screen to a grid layout. "Apparently there were more Opposition forces there than we anticipated. We're in the process of moving more stock into their main distribution centers. Communication channels are clear. So far unimpeded and not hacked. We don't anticipate that to last for long, though. Days, maybe hours."

The president turned to the left side of the room and addressed a young woman seated in the corner, hunched over a bank of floating BC5 screens in an arc around her.

"How long?" he asked her.

Next to me, Armise leaned forward to see who the president was talking to. Apparently, despite being the person who had given us the coordinates of how to find her, Armise had never met Chen Ying.

Her long black hair with wild streaks of blue and crimson whipped around as she turned in her chair. She was tiny, even in comparison to Jegs or the president. Her face was round, with prominent angular cheekbones, full lips and piercing green eyes that gave her a near predatory appearance. If it wasn't for those eyes she could have been viewed as the child she was. Neveed had told me she was sixteen. I doubted that was true.

"Hours," she answered with authority and hunched over her screens again.

"The key," I whispered into Armise's ear, using Chen's nickname to clue him in.

He lifted an eyebrow in silent question—not making the connection with what I was telling him.

"Chen Ying. The key."

A tip from Armise had sent us searching for her ten years ago, and none of us had expected to find a child prodigy instead of the actual encryption chip. But her inherent mathematical genius had been exactly what the Revolution needed to begin cracking open the infochip. Like me, Chen had been brought into war at a very young age. Unlike me, she had made a home here in the capital and with the members of the Revolution.

He sat back against the wall. "Huh."

I'd had the same reaction when I'd first met her.

At the front of the room Neveed continued his debriefing. Armise started to ask me another question and I waved him off, trying to listen in over the cacophony, because I couldn't have just heard what I thought had come out of Neveed's mouth.

"What was that, Neveed?" I said, loud enough for heads to snap in my direction.

The room went silent.

Neveed faced me, his face an emotionless mask. "The stadium was destroyed by a reverb. Ahriman Blanc ordered the strike after your shot."

My stomach dropped.

I couldn't believe that what I was hearing was the truth. A reverberation bomb. The same type that had brought down the building I'd been born in. Where my parents had reportedly died and my legs had nearly been crushed. They were the most destructive of modern bombs—ever since the nuclear arsenals had been destroyed in an effort to civilize the mass destruction wrought by the Borders War.

I leaned on the bar in front of the last row of seats. "How soon after?" I was nearly growling, the implications settling in and a red haze of anger to overtaking my vision. It had been less than twenty minutes since my shot, so I knew the answer wouldn't be good.

Neveed narrowed his eyes, tipped his chin up but didn't reply. I knew him well enough to tell that he didn't want to give me the answer.

"How the fuck long after?" I challenged.

Neveed glanced at Armise, his lips pursing, then ground out, "Immediately."

Which meant two things. First, that Ahriman had either been aware of what I was going to do or he had planned this assault regardless of the outcome of my shot. But more importantly, more sickeningly, it meant that everyone inside who hadn't had a transport chip—every average citizen and child who had been trying to escape the chaos created by my shot—had been instantaneously obliterated.

Hundreds of thousands of people. Gone.

Because of my shot.

I gave my head a shake, clearing the thought out and reforming my view on the attack. No. They weren't dead because of me. They'd been unceremoniously exterminated by Ahriman Blanc and the Opposition.

"Any survivors?" Simion asked from my right.

Neveed flicked his hand over the controls and brought up an aerial feed of the destruction. "It's early, but all indications are there are no survivors. We haven't been able to pick up any life signs from the dronebot scans."

The president gave a signal to cut the screens, the scenes of devastation snapping off into black. Above our heads and over the mournful silence that hung in the control room, the bombs continued to explode, the staccato rattle of gunfire echoing in the stone chamber.

The president paused, surveying each reaction. He stepped to the front of the room and faced everyone. His features were twisted in rage—lips pursed, jaw grinding, his eyebrows furrowed into a deep vee. His practiced, resonant voice sounded deathly calm when he spoke. "We had one victory today. One of many to come. The Premiere of Singapore and decades-long leader of the Opposition has been eliminated. But, as you can see, there is no time to rest on that success. Your fellow citizens are out there fighting and dying right now, while we stand here protected. Safe." His nostrils flared and his voice picked up, betraying the depth of his fury in a rare show of unchecked emotion. "Don't worry. You all will have your chance to fight. For now we have jobs to do to prepare us all for that moment. Do you have anything new, Chen?"

She didn't bother to hide an irritated stare as she raised her head. "You'll know when I do."

Next to me Armise blew out a breath that I recognized as a restrained expression of disbelief. That there was anyone in the world who would dare to talk to the president with such forwardness, let alone complete dismissal of his deadly reputation, had been shocking to me at first as well.

But if Chen's brusque manner had affected the president—now or ever—then he didn't show it outwardly. The president pointed at Neveed. "I want an aircomm with each continental general in twenty minutes. Full status updates. Approximate casualty counts. Weapons reports. How well the munitions are holding. And status on our shield capabilities."

"Shields?" Armise asked. It was the first time he'd spoken out loud to anyone besides Jegs or me.

The president didn't hesitate to answer him. "The Opposition is still using sonicrifles, pistols and reverbs. As long as we can keep our shields up and operational we'll be able to protect our forces better than they will theirs. Therefore we expect them to adapt and attack the shield generators and battery stores next."

"Where do the Nationalists stand in this?" Simion asked. But I knew he wasn't asking for his benefit. Jegs' stiffened almost imperceptibly. It was a question she had a personal stake in but wouldn't dare voice, no matter how much she wanted the answer.

The president faced Simion and kept his gaze off Jegs. "Grimshaw has notified us they're going to stand back and let us fight this out. They're neutral."

Neveed and I might have been the only people in the room who could read the underlying disdain in the president's answer.

I crossed my arms. "Are we going to engage them?" This was a decision that needed immediate and definitive resolution, as it would impact every tactic from here on out.

"Not yet," the president answered. He waved in my direction, addressing the entire room again. "For those of you who have only seen that face on screen or in operational reports, this is Colonel Merq Grayson. Next to him, Armise Darcan. They are—" The president hesitated, the lift of his eyebrow making my throat clench as I waited to hear how he was going to finish that sentence.

What were we?

Armise wasn't a Dark Ops officer for Singapore anymore. He would be considered a traitor in his country—which was primarily Opposition territory.

My mission was over. I hadn't been in active combat as a Peacemaker in ten years now.

Our current roles were undefined until the president decided to set me, or us, on another mission. I had to consider the possibility that whatever target I would be unleashed on next, I would have Armise at my side instead of my usual crew of Simion or Jegs.

The realization was jarring. I didn't know where Armise stood on this, but for me it solidified the reality that Armise had inexplicably become my only true ally. We were alone in this together. That was not a comforting consideration.

The president continued, "Merq and Armise are the reason the Revolution has been able to take this monumental step. Don't bother getting to know them well though. Despite the prevalent coverage of that shot"—he turned toward us with that all-knowing smile I most associated with him—"you won't be seeing much of them."

Armise and I looked at each other. Armise lifted an eyebrow and I shrugged. I had no idea what the president was talking about. Armise grumbled quietly, the muscles in his jaw working.

"Now let's get back to work," the president instructed. The noise level kicked up and masked the sound of the battle being waged above ground.

Neveed motioned for me from the front of the room, then waved Armise off, gesturing toward the president. The president pulled Armise to the side as I continued forward.

I watched warily over my shoulder as the president put an arm on Armise's biceps and Armise leaned down to listen. Then the president slipped something into Armise's hand.

"Going to have to fight to keep your attention from now on," Neveed said matter-of-factly, drawing my attention back to him.

I eyed him. We might have been on more civil terms now that we were no longer working together, but the damage done by years of mistrust and hidden agendas wouldn't be wiped away in a day. Possibly not ever. No matter how much truth he purported to feed to me, I didn't believe that Neveed was capable of setting aside his personal feelings for me from the needs of the cause. Shit, or his own grandiose need for the power to hold the unknown over me. I didn't doubt for a second that he would use me for his purposes—personal or tactical—without thought to what I wanted.

If Neveed could sense my annoyance, he ignored it. "We'll have more targets for you." He tipped his head in Armise's direction. "For both of you. But not yet."

"Next, you find your parents," the president said as he appeared at my side with Armise.

I hesitated. Ahriman had attempted to buy my compliance by kidnapping my parents, but his desired outcome had been the opposite. Now they were being held by the Opposition, but I couldn't believe that was where my skills were most needed.

I addressed the president and not Neveed. "Respectfully, sir, I think my talents are better utilized in something else besides recovering my parents. If they are even alive."

"They are alive. And recovering them is not a suggestion, it's an order. But we're not ready to move on their location yet. Eat something. Get cleaned up.

Sleep for a couple hours. You did your job. Let us do ours."

His tone was more fatherly than authoritarian, but that made it even clearer that his plan wasn't up for discussion.

"We have quarters set up for you in my wing. Dinner in the galley." The president smiled at Armise. "Coffee, too."

Armise gave a clipped nod, but I saw the set of his shoulders relax.

I'd never seen him look more human.

Chapter Two

"Rest? Is he fucking kidding?" I said under my breath as soon as Armise and I exited the control room.

Armise walked shoulder to shoulder with me as one of the president's guards led us through the tunnels.

"He's right, Merq. Even you have to sleep and eat."

I pointed to the ceiling and gripped his arm, dragging him to a stop. "Do you hear that? Do you? Those are bombs. Gunfire. The Revolution is happening now. Right the fuck now. And he's ordering me to rest?"

The guard stopped with us, keeping a respectful distance.

Armise extracted his arm from my hold. "This will not be resolved tonight, whether we fight or not. That, up there, is the initial wave of battle. You know that. You take to your bed when you can. You get food when you can. You appreciate shelter and blankets and a warm, filling meal. Because you never know when any of those options will become scarce. Or worse, you will be dead."

I wanted to argue with him, but I held my tongue. Armise made too much sense. I motioned for the guard to continue.

The guard led us through a series of concrete corridors with closed-off doors and people speaking in hushed tones as they passed us. We got questioning glances and a series of wary eyes studying us but never acknowledging our presence with any friendly overtures. Which was more than acceptable to me. At one time my size had been enough to turn heads, and combined with the even more massive frame of Armise next to me, and our unmistakable faces, I knew people were going to be more curious than not.

I was going to have to learn how to fucking deal with this level of public recognition. Maybe Dr. Casas would be up for some impromptu facial scrambling during my forced downtime.

I was used to being covert, underground in all senses of the word, known to my enemies but to very few of my allies. All that had started changing in the public spectacle in preparation for the Olympics. With my shot and the expansive media attention there would be no escaping recognition anymore.

The guard stopped at a door and held it open for us. Armise crossed the threshold first and a burst of warm air and the scent of fresh food greeted us as we entered the galley.

The door slammed shut behind us and Armise crossed to a table, settling into a seat with the same grace he always exhibited despite his size. I huffed into a chair across from him. My stomach growled and Armise gave a gruff laugh.

I stared at him, the sound of his rumbling response rolling through me. Three times I'd heard Armise laugh now, but this time it was…lighthearted? Before I thought of anything to say, a heaped plate was being placed in front of me, and one in Armise's waiting hands.

"Didn't think I'd ever see you again," a voice came from behind me.

I shifted and looked warily over my shoulder, unsure of whom to expect. I was greeted with the lopsided, easy grin of a thin man with bushy, wild hair plaited into braids that nearly reached his waist.

I pointed to the plate. "Crimean sauce, Exley? You should know better."

Exley swiped the plate away with a grin. "The hero of the Revolution shall have whatever he wishes."

Armise already had half his food downed. "A friend of yours?"

"No," Exley answered as he set a fresh plate—without the offensive faux meat sauce this time—with a clatter in front of me. "Merq doesn't have friends."

"No friends who try to feed me swill," I retorted.

Exley clasped my shoulder. "Still don't understand how you keep that body so buff without ingesting one piece of meat."

I pointed a fork at Armise's plate. "That is not meat. I remember what real animals taste like, son."

Exley gave a rolling laugh, then a slap on my back and retreated behind a door that had to be the kitchen.

"I don't eat that chemically processed shit," I explained to Armise.

Armise shrugged and shoveled more food in as I grimaced.

"Everything is genetmod," he mumbled around a full mouth.

I started at his flippant response, then waited to see if he would continue.

I'd always suspected Armise himself was genetmod, but it wasn't like we'd ever sat down and had a heart-to-heart, let alone a conversation about the genetically manipulated advantages that made us uniquely superior to unmodified citizens.

I studied Armise, searching for any hint to the meaning behind his words. But he kept eating as if he made no connection between the food in front of him and his own body. Maybe he didn't.

I didn't bother to reply.

I was suspicious about how genetmod the man across from me was, but that wasn't a topic I had interest in exploring at the moment. This was definitely not a conversation for now. Maybe not ever. Especially if the choice was between talking and clearing everything off the plate in front of me. My mouth watered and my stomach rumbled again. I couldn't remember the last meal I'd eaten while seated at a table. And a hot one at that.

Exley could cook. But I'd never tell him that.

While Exley might have been the best cook I'd encountered in my years as a Peacemaker, it wasn't often I had the chance to eat any of his food. And not just because I was out on missions more than I was in the States. Exley was a citizen of the tent camps and not a Revolution soldier nor in any way officially tied to the president's agenda, even though he'd been working in States' facilities since I was a teenager.

I remembered him as a child—dark skin free from the dust and grime of the camps because he was obsessive about cleanliness. His impressive braids had started as oiled locks pulled back into plaits against his scalp, keeping the curling, stray hairs from blowing loose as he maneuvered around the kitchen and dining areas of the Peacemaker headquarters.

His deeper involvement with the Revolution had started because Simion and I were bored, as only teenagers in the midst of a war could be. We'd bribed Exley with a military-issue knife we knew he would be able to trade on the black market for him to show us how to sneak out of the barracks and into the city.

Exley knew the capital better than anyone I'd met. He could roam the tunnels and alleys without a map. He knew the layout of buildings as if he'd traversed their hallways for years. He knew people, and everyone seemed to know him. Yet when he wanted to, Exley could pass through a crowd without ever being noticed.

It was those skills—discovered by Simion and I on the multiple jaunts through the city Exley led us on—that had made me approach Neveed about the possibility of bringing Exley fully into Revolution dealings.

Exley was correct in his assessment that I wouldn't have called him a friend, but that didn't mean I didn't respect him. I just knew Exley would give me shit if I ever complimented him on anything. Our relationship was one that had never quite moved out of the contentious but companionable sarcasm and one-upmanship of teenagers discovering their roles in the world.

Regardless of how close we had been at one time, over the years Exley and I had spent less and less time together. His last assignment had kept him on the move—trading messages between the president and the safe house where my parents were located.

Had been located, I corrected myself.

They were never supposed to have left the shelter of that house on the outskirts of the capital. But for some reason they had chosen to abandon the one place they couldn't be harmed and put themselves directly in the path of Ahriman and the Opposition—making it my job to get them back.

My frustration didn't wane even as my belly filled. Armise and I sat silently at the table, the sounds of warfare crackling above us. We avoided eye contact, avoided speaking to each other. It was the first time we'd been relatively alone since the tunnels under the stadium where Armise had confessed his involvement with the Revolution and that he had done it all to protect me. And wasn't that just the last fucking thing in the world I wanted to discuss. Like feeling his arm around me on that transport platform after the shot, it all felt too intimate.

As if I knew what real intimacy felt like.

Armise pushed his empty plate away, grabbed the steaming cup of coffee into his hands and rested his elbows on the table. He didn't bother waiting for me to finish before he said, "You have no desire to make sure your parents make it out of this alive?"

The fork stopped partway to my lips. "My parents gave me nothing."

"Life. For a cause that you believe in."

I dropped my fork, pushed away from the table and crossed my arms. "We're going to have a heart-to-heart?"

Armise sipped his coffee. "You going to stay in this shit mood?"

I ran my fingers through my hair and mumbled, "I can't sit here anymore. Exley." The door to the kitchen swung open and his head appeared around the corner, braids swinging. "They have a gym here?"

Exley nodded. "Full training facility one floor down. Weapons range as well. You want me to take you?"

I shook my head and nearly sent my chair halfway across the room with how fast I got up. "I'll find it."

I didn't wait for Armise. Didn't extend an invite for him to join me. I was too restless. That feeling of too close, too much, was grinding away at me each second I was forced to look into Armise's steely gaze and begin to refit the pieces of our convoluted fate back together in a way that could make sense.

It only took one question to a woman scurrying through the hallway—as if she was desperately trying to get as far away from me as possible—to find the stairs down to the lower level. True to Exley's words, most of the lower level appeared to be a stocked training facility.

I was standing in the center of the room debating the benefits of working off some aggression with either weights or guns when the door snicked open and Armise entered without a knock.

I glared at him. "Listen, Darcan. I don't need you following me around here as if I'm expected to entertain you. This truce or whatever it is between us changes very little."

Armise chuckled. Low and derisive. "Is that right? Are you telling me there is not even a part of you that is beginning to trust me? A part of you that wonders why you are so fucking smart and capable yet it took so long for you to figure out what was actually going on? Open your eyes for once, Merq, and focus on something besides yourself. This 'whatever' between us changes everything. And if you are too self-absorbed and petulant to see it then I've wasted the last thirteen years of my life."

Petulant and self-absorbed? Right. As if I were a child who Armise had been sent to mind.

"Fuck you," I answered and went for the weights.

I slid the weights over a barbell—maxing out the amount I could press—and lay back on the bench.

Armise came up behind me and stood with his arms crossed.

I positioned my hands around the bar. "I believe I said fuck you."

"And that is supposed to be my cue to leave? It is as if you do not know me at all."

"Do I?"

Armise motioned to the bar, for me to start. "Not really," he answered with an honesty that surprised me.

I hesitated for only a second, then grabbed the bar and lifted it from the machine. I made the reps slow, inching the bar nearly to my chest and back again while Armise watched. I tried to ignore his presence, to forget that he was so close, but even with the focus it took to press the weights off me I couldn't push him out of my mind.

My muscles began to quake under the heavy weights, warmth spreading through me, endorphins kicking in. I tracked my progress by the shaking of my muscles instead of by a predetermined number of sets. My heartbeat pounded in my ears, sweat rolled down my temple and I fought to keep my back and legs unmoving as my arms tired. The adrenaline served only to hype me up more.

This nervous energy had to go. And I was going to do whatever was necessary to drive it—and him—from my mind.

"I don't need a fucking babysitter," I gritted out between reps.

Armise walked away without saying a word—I sensed him moving out of my orbit rather than seeing it. I didn't know if my ability to track him was due to my training or something more primal. If there was anything I'd come to terms with over our thirteen years, it was that being with him was an instinct and a drive I hadn't been born with but existed deep within me nonetheless. He fueled my aggression, my frustration. He made me uneasy and left me unhinged. And I couldn't deny anymore that that might have been the reason I was so drawn to him. There was little that affected me anymore.

But he still did.

A mechanical hum and the thump of heavy steps came from the corner of the room. I put the bar back in place and sat up, my elbows on my knees as I caught my breath. Armise ran on the moving floor beneath him, his fingers working over the transparent screen, adjusting speed, incline and resistance. His back was to me, his shirt and shoes discarded to the side, his tattoos flexing with the movement of his shoulders and back, his breathing even as his bare feet pounded the machine. Most likely testing the limits of what it could handle.

Always testing the limits of what I could handle.

I swallowed thickly and swiped the sweat from my brow and above my lips. I thought about our last encounter, in that tunnel, me driving into him harshly. Without regard to what he could or couldn't physically take.

Never enough. No matter how many times, it was never enough. He was my greatest weakness. My addiction even when the ability to resist temptation should've been beaten out of me by the PsychHAgs.

And now he wasn't going anywhere.

I pulled my piercing between my teeth and openly watched him run. Appreciated would be a more appropriate word. Leered would be more accurate.

He was strength of will embodied. A testament to training, hard work and singular focus. Much like me, he had been molded by his government into what and who he was today. But unlike me, that had never seemed to be his primary motivation.

My thoughts skittered back to his confession that I didn't really know who he was. I understood his battle tactics. Could read him better than some of the soldiers I'd fought with for years. I knew his history from classified files and from the little Armise had willingly told me over the last thirteen years.

Thirteen fucking years since he'd kissed me in that warehouse in Singapore.

And it still wasn't enough.

Chapter Three

Why the fuck was I even trying to fight this?

I didn't just want to touch him. It was a physical need. I needed my mind to still, and the only time it ever fully did was right after I'd fucked Armise. In those minutes, lost in him, for him, and in the seconds after. When I was solely aware of his body and mine. Of the movement of muscle and bone. Of tongues and teeth. His hands. Hot breath and uncontrollable moans.

The floor shook from the falls of his feet on the moving section of the floor and with deep reverberations as bombs continued to fall above us. The continual movement unnerved me. This sensation was unlike anything I'd ever experienced before. I'd been in active battle, but sonic weapons surged then pulsed—an audible pop and hiss of waves piercing the air. Even when a reverb was dropped there was no real explosion, more of an implosion and collapsing of whatever had been struck.

I crossed the room. Armise didn't turn as I approached, but I knew he sensed me approaching. He always knew where I was. If I'd given it much thought before today, I'd probably have considered it the watchfulness and wariness that comes with tracking your enemies. But now I was rethinking everything. Re-evaluating our time together through the lens of confession and hidden loyalties.

He'd been the one to save me in the DCR, to make sure I made it back to the States alive. And he'd been the one who had gotten me out of the stadium after shooting the premiere when I'd been sure I was going to die.

He'd told me he couldn't live without me anymore. That he wouldn't. I didn't know what to do with that. With him.

Shit.

He really wasn't going anywhere. So I was going to have to find some way to deal with this.

But right now, my body was itching to move. I didn't have any orders besides to rest up and wait. My next mission was to rescue my parents—two people who I hadn't seen in person in almost three decades. Their presence had always been more theoretical than real, their influence over me nonexistent.

I was closer to Armise than I would ever be to them. And yet it would be my next job to risk my life to bring them back to the president.

Their place in the Revolution was one of myth—not unlike my grandfather, who had invented the sonicbullet. Their supposed deaths had been viewed as martyrdom for the cause. They were part of the original rebels who had formed the Revolution. Contemporaries of the president. Friends even. If any such thing existed anymore.

I stepped onto the section of floor next to Armise and hit the button on the screen that activated in front of me, the floor sliding effortlessly into fluid movement. I quickly matched and exceeded Armise's pace.

I outpaced him, nearly two footfalls for every one of his. My nervous energy dissipated, but only by the tiniest of fractions. Every crunch and rumble from the bombs overhead drove the peace from me. Every shuddering crack of the walls, the ceiling shaking like it could cave at any moment, jangled my nerves.

That we were underground didn't help the situation. I wasn't claustrophobic, but I'd been trained well enough to understand with complete clarity the dangerousness of a place with limited exit options.

I preferred being above ground. I was at my strongest in an urban environment. I didn't fare well in the wilds—forest, desert or water. I didn't understand nature, even the little that was left of it. Most of the world had been turned to wasteland during the Borders War, and our current use of artillery would only further that change. We were destroying our planet, but that consideration had long since been studied, debated and rejected in favor of the destruction that came with fighting for our cause.

I couldn't shake my anxiety, no matter how fast or hard I ran. I clicked the speed up until my breaths were coming in forced huffs, sweat dripping from my brow. Faster, harder, I had to drive the thoughts from my head. I needed a mission. A purpose. And right now, I had none.

Armise swiped his hand over the screen, shutting the moving floor down, and yanked me off the machine, setting me off balance. I tumbled away from him and he pulled me into his grasp, his arms snaking around my waist. His lips grazed my neck, his breath hot against my skin.

"What do you need?" he whispered into my ear.

His touch grounded me, brought me back to my senses with jolting clarity.

I looked back at him, licked my lips. How had he known I needed anything?

"Not here," I said, pointing to the corners of the room where the cameras were probably located. "Too many eyes. Neveed will have made sure our quarters are free of surveillance."

I pulled out of his arms and went for the door. I didn't wait to see if he followed me. I knew he would.

As I passed by the galley, I popped my head inside. "Exley!"

Exley emerged from the back room and cocked an eyebrow in reply.

"Where are our rooms?"

"Last two to the right. Not sure…"

I didn't hear the rest of what he said because I was already on the move again.

I stopped at the door that was second from last, twisted the doorknob and hesitated before opening it.

Exley had said there were two rooms set up for us. One for me and one for Armise. But there was no way in fuck I was letting him go anywhere else. I needed this. I needed him.

Now.

Armise came up next to me and leaned against the wall, his arms crossed. He'd put his shirt back on sometime between the training facility and here, yet his apparent modesty did nothing but grate at me more.

"Do we need to…?"

"What?" I snapped.

Armise's jaw ticked as he restrained a smile. "The same room?"

"I'm not asking you to move in with me," I erupted. I wasn't sure whether my sudden surge of anger had more to do with him or me.

"I am the traitor."

"Right. And I'm the hero of the Revolution. Didn't you hear that?"

"Perception matters, Merq."

I knew what he was saying, but I couldn't have cared less.

"Fuck that." I threw the door open and motioned for him to come in. "I have nothing to hide."

* * * *

The door slammed definitively behind me.

I was sealing my fate, probably had long before this moment, but there was something about this exact scenario that gave me pause. I was in a Revolution stronghold, the president and my fellow Peacemakers only steps away. And Armise was with me. Without fear of discovery. Without fear of retribution or death.

With me instead of against me.

The ground shook beneath my feet again and I had to close my eyes to shut down the sensation that the world I knew was crumbling around me.

"I've never seen you this unsettled." Armise's voice came from the other side of the room.

I took a deep breath and scrubbed my hands through my hair. I could feel Armise moving toward me, his normally silent footfalls thudding against the carpet as if he was warning me that he was coming. When I looked up he was only inches from me, the inherent coldness of his body filling the air around us.

"What do you need, Merq?" he repeated, this time in a much firmer voice. Demanding an answer.

I didn't know how to answer him. I couldn't cut through the static in my head, or the reverberations of the bombs dropping above us. I needed him to take it all away. And it scared me that I knew he could if he wanted to. If I asked him to.

He put his hand against my neck, drawing me into his body, and I obeyed, moving because his touch ordered me to.

"Fucking breathe, Merq. Breathe," he reminded me as he locked his gaze to mine.

His eyes were blue in the low light. Dark. In shadow.

His lips set in a thin line. Frowning. As he studied me.

There was pity in the set of his features and that, more than any other emotion, I wouldn't stand for.

I broke away and pushed him off me. I stripped my clothes off as I moved. I needed to fuck him. To regain control of my jangled nerves. To wrest this thing between us into something I could understand again.

Nothing in my life made sense and I didn't deal well with uncertainty.

"On the bed."

Armise lifted his shirt off and tossed it to the side. He rolled his shoulders and slowly unbuttoned his pants, his eyes never leaving mine.

I dropped onto the bed and unlaced my boots, discarding them with a thump against the dresser.

Armise appeared in front of me and positioned himself between my knees. He carded his hand through my hair and to my neck, drawing my cheek to his stomach. He was naked and the hair of his legs and stomach rasped against my skin as I trailed my hands over his hips and down his thighs. I inhaled, taking in the scent of him, a smell unlike any other man I'd ever been with—masculine, intoxicating, heady. A scent that would forever be associated with dirty floors, back alleys, foreign beds, stolen minutes and rebellion.

His skin was cold—as it always was—chilling me, comforting me.

Fuck. When had I become this deeply entwined with him?

I wrapped my arms around his waist and pulled him to the bed, turning him onto his back, slotting my body over his. I moved roughly against him, my hands grasping, digging into his muscles, my lips and tongue seeking out the taste of his skin. He pushed at my waistband, sliding my pants over my hips. I stood, dropping my pants to the floor and stepping out of them as I surveyed his massive frame—naked, vulnerable, stretched out and taking up the width of the bed. I licked my lips and watched him stroke himself.

I couldn't deal with the slowness of his movements, with the deliberate teasing of his hand over his cock. My body vibrated with the need to pound into him, to be inside him. To conquer him and quiet the demons stirring in my head.

"Turn over," I ordered through clenched teeth.

His lips curled into a snarl. "No."

I stopped undressing, anger flaring inside me.

He sat up and brought an arm around me, toppling me into the bed. He flipped me over and put his full weight on me, pinning me.

"Just stop," Armise commanded. "Shut the fuck up. Be still."

I fought the urge to move. I wanted to push him off me. He held onto me tighter, bringing his body in line with mine. He let go of my arm and brought his left hand to my face—that hand with the missing finger I'd taken from him—and traced the line of my lips.

"Breathe," he said again, this time with quiet force.

I relaxed my muscles and sank into the mattress, allowing the familiarity of his touch to envelop me. It was only then, as the minutes dragged on and there were no further vibrations radiating from the floor, that I realized the bombs had stopped.

"How long has it been this quiet?"

His hold on me relaxed. "Not long."

"Do you think it's over?" I asked, knowing the answer before the question was fully out of my mouth. I cringed. I did sound like a fucking child.

This was war. And it was only beginning. I would take the respite while it lasted, even if the quiet likely meant a rallying of Opposition forces.

"For now," Armise answered distractedly. He pushed himself off me, rolling to the side.

I ignored the defiant set of Armise's shoulders and the way he purposefully kept any part of his body from touching mine. Whatever was going on in Armise's head was more than I could handle at the moment. My body and mind were wrecked. The stress of the last two days came crashing down on me all at once as silence filled the room.

I was naked and he was naked. But I was too tired to care. Too exhausted to move.

I threw my forearm over my eyes and took a deep breath.

I didn't know what time of day it was and wasn't sure if it even mattered. The days leading up to the opening ceremonies felt like eons ago. Another lifetime. So much had changed in such a short time that I was struggling to keep up. A mission years in the planning and it had taken one fraction of a second to end. With the death of the leader of the Opposition I had set the Revolution on its collision course with history. I'd reignited the Borders War and signed my own death warrant. I knew with the certainty of the damned that I was the most wanted man on the planet at this very moment.

My name and my face were known worldwide and I would be a target for the mere fact that I'd been doing my job. My death would be a prize coveted by those who wanted to see the Revolution fail. And I had to consider that there might be some Revolutionaries who would want to see me dead as well. A martyr to the cause. It was an undeniable fact of war—nothing brought people together more than a death to mourn and avenge.

I was going to have to be infinitely more careful now. I was relatively sure who I could trust—the president, Neveed, Jegs, Simion. And Armise. Him more than anyone else. But even as the thought crossed my mind it left an unsettling wake of emotion.

The mattress dipped and bounced back as Armise got up. I lifted my arm and watched him prowl out of the bedroom and into the en suite. I scooted back on the bed and lifted the blanket, crawling under the soft gray material. I needed to sleep while there was time. But my brain wouldn't shut down.

Armise emerged from the bathroom, wiping his hands on a white cloth. He stopped at the edge of the bed, threw the towel into a corner and climbed in next to me, burrowing under the covers without a word. He turned on his side, baring his back to me.

My eyes trailed over the thick black lines of the tattoos crisscrossing his skin. Loops and whirls of a language I could speak but couldn't read. Jagged edges that framed battle scars. Most of Armise's back was covered in ink.

I reached out and traced the thickest line—a solid black slash, almost like a lightning bolt—that marked the spot where I'd cut him in the DCR standoff. A violent struggle that I'd nearly died from. A confrontation that had ended with Armise saving my life. He had three permanent marks from that encounter—his missing finger, the scar and this tattoo.

Armise didn't respond to my uninvited touch. His shoulders rose and fell as he breathed in and out slowly. He was covered in external marks that documented the years of his life. And I couldn't help but think back to his words that he wouldn't go on without me anymore. Perhaps I had marked him in ways that couldn't be seen with the human eye.

I didn't know what that meant for us. There was some part of me that recognized the weight of that statement and heard the ferocity of his proclamation. But I couldn't—or maybe wouldn't—put a name to who he was to me.

The only other person in my life who dared to show any similar depth of emotion toward me was the president. He was a father to me more than my own.

"I don't love them," I whispered before I even realized I was speaking the thought out loud. I drew my hand back and waited for Armise to respond.

Minutes went by with Armise's back still to me, and I began to think that he was asleep, then, "They are your parents."

Of course Armise would know what I was talking about, even when I wasn't sure. I flopped onto my back and stared at the ceiling.

"It doesn't matter."

Armise sat up against the headboard and stared down at me, his steely eyes boring a hole through me. "It does. People need love, Merq. Why else fight?"

I scoffed. "Duty? Loyalty? Pride? There are many reasons that have nothing to do with that emotion."

Armise frowned.

I threw the covers off me, sat up and put one foot on the floor. I was ready to bolt. I didn't know what was happening in Armise's head and I had zero interest in trying to pick apart his words. Nothing good could come of this conversation. Why had I even brought up my parents?

"Like I said, it doesn't matter." I dismissed the thought with a wave of my hand. "If the president wants me to bring them back then I will."

"A soldier first," Armise answered dryly.

Frustration coiled in my gut. I turned on him, letting loose a sneer. "What else is there?"

Armise crossed his arms. "You have spent so much time in the dark that you forget what the light looks like."

I pointed at him. "And you remember? Don't bullshit me, Armise. You are a product of war as much as I am. We were thrust into this existence, but that doesn't mean we weren't made for it. That darkness isn't just a part of us—it's who we are. I've seen you kill. I know what you're capable of. Both of us, Armise—both of us—are more animal than human."

Armise tipped his chin in a defiant stance. "I know what I am."

"A soldier first," I spat back at him.

Armise shook his head. "My skill with a rifle does not define me."

I pushed off the bed and faced him, satisfied that anger was overtaking me. This I could understand. "So what does? Your ability to survive? That you breathe and move and think? None of that makes us human—it just proves that we're alive. Able to go into battle one more time. Again and again until death finally releases us from this hell. Don't fool yourself. We exist to kill.

To be the darkness that descends and wipes out hope. Others are meant to be leaders and to strive for a greater good, but not us. We cover our hands in blood so the righteous can disavow any knowledge of the evils that must occur for there to be peace. And in our world, if you're not behind the rifle, you're in front of it."

My body shook. How could Armise not see this? I didn't love my parents because that emotion wouldn't help me on the battlefield. I wasn't human. I couldn't be if it was this easy to take another life. And my darkness was the only part of myself that I fully understood and accepted. That darkness gave me purpose.

Without a purpose I was nothing.

I ran my fingers through my hair and spoke out loud, more to myself than to him. "Fuck. I can't do this."

I dropped back onto the bed, turned my back to him and threw the sheets over my still-naked body. I closed my eyes and repeated my mantra until the images on my eyelids were a jumbled menagerie of Chemsense clouds, a desperate grip on Armise's arm, sonicrifle pops, the *click-thunk* of a chambered bullet and a weeping child with battered legs whom I lifted and carried from the swirling dust of a reverb explosion…

There was a knock at the door that woke me from sleep, my dreams wiping away, disappearing into the ether as my eyes flew open.

I didn't know how long I'd been asleep—minutes? Hours?—but I wasn't any more rested than I'd been before collapsing into the mattress in frustration. I was alone in bed, a sheet thrown haphazardly around my hips. Armise sat in a chair across from me, the blue wash of a BC5 screen illuminating his face.

"What is it?" Armise answered the knock with annoyance.

The door opened and Neveed stood in profile, the light from the hallway shadowing his face as he said, "The president wants to see you, Merq."

Chapter Four

I knocked on the dark wood panel door—so out of place amid the stone, concrete and synthetic materials in this wing of the bunker—and waited for permission to enter. Instead the door creaked open as I tapped my knuckles against it, revealing a room with low lighting and wood walls the same texture and shade as the door.

"Come in, Merq." The president's voice came from the part of the room still hidden from my view.

I stepped into the room and surveyed the bizarre interior.

"Is it real?" I asked. I couldn't resist running a hand over the wall. It was unlike anything I'd seen before, with a depth and richness of color—shades of brown and gold too vivid to be manufactured—that I'd never seen in faux panels.

The president nodded. "Reclaimed. You've never seen wood displayed like this before?"

"In person? No."

The president cocked his head and studied me.

"I've never been here," I reminded him.

He made a gruff noise of acknowledgment. "I forget just how deep undercover you've been for most of your life."

My eyes were drawn to the wall next to where the president sat behind a desk of molded synthetic polymaterials—in stark contrast to the warm and antiquated feel of the rest of the room. Over the glossy material of the desk, the president's BC5 screen flickered.

I moved without thought to the object on the wall, drawn to study it further. Framed under a dim light, sputtering with the effort to stay illuminated, there was a long rectangular press of rusted metal, the paint faded. It was a cross touched by the wear of time. The words across the surface were raised as if they'd been punched into the fragile material from the back.

Blessed are the peacemakers, for they shall be called sons of God.

I ran my fingers over the metal relief, the edges sharp, catching on the tips of my callused fingers.

"It's where you got the name from, didn't you?" I immediately connected the relic with the term the president had given to the soldiers for the States.

Out of the corner of my eye I could see the president nod. "But not out of respect."

I snorted. Of course it hadn't been. The president had reformed the military branch after usurping leadership of the Continental States over thirty years ago. The Peacemakers, his real soldiers—the ones he trusted the most and relied on—were like me. We were soldiers for the Revolution, not just the forces assembled from civilians to protect the borders and interest of the country.

"You're too intellectual for this job," I mused. I stood at the end of his desk, studying his black uniform with the bright orange sunburst on the shoulder instead of the traditional States' insignia. "New uniform?"

"You'll find yours in your closet."

I stood in front of him and waited. I didn't know why he'd called for me. It was likely to discuss my next orders or to debrief on my shot, but for once I wasn't sure. Regardless of why he wanted to speak to me, there were things I wanted to know. But I'd never been in a position to demand answers from him, and now was no different. I trusted the president, was closer to him than any other person except Armise, but that didn't make our relationship easy or friendly.

I set my feet, crossed my arms and cracked my neck. The president sat perched on his chair, waiting for me to break our silent standoff.

"How long did you know about Armise?" I finally asked.

"That's not what you really want to know."

I crooked an eyebrow, but didn't concede that he was correct in his assessment.

"You want to know if it changes anything about how I view you," the president said.

I should have hesitated to admit this to him. If it was anybody else I would have. But the president knew me.

"And does it?"

"No," he replied. With a wave of his hand he dismissed the screen from his desktop.

I believed him. The president had never tried to bullshit me and I saw no reason for him to start now. I pulled out the chair and sat down to face him, waiting for him to get to whatever he had called me for.

The president's chair squeaked in protest at his paunchy frame as he shifted. "Armise didn't know who Chen was."

It wasn't a question, but I answered anyway. "Apparently not."

"He wasn't acting?"

"No," I said with surety.

The president considered this then leaned forward, steepling his fingers. "You may want to talk to Feliu."

The States' doctor? Dr. Feliu Casas was the primary physician for the president. The same one who had been at my bedside when I'd emerged from my two-month-long coma after the DCR standoff and had inserted my chips.

"Why?" Although I had a good idea where this was going.

"He was able to run some tests on Armise through the transport. There were some unusual findings."

"We already knew he was genetmod," I replied, acknowledging out loud my long-held belief that Armise had been subjected—either willingly or unwillingly—to the process of taking his base DNA structure and manipulating it to enhance his strengths.

"True," the president said. "But we didn't know the extent."

"And?"

"It's extensive."

I whistled under my breath and sat back in my chair. Fuck. There was no way I would have known for sure without the scan through our transport into the bunker. Armise had never admitted to being genetmod. It was possible he wasn't aware of how significant the changes were that his government had forced upon him. But extensive genetmods would explain his cold skin, that his core temperature seemed to be degrees lower than should be viable for human survival.

That wasn't my greatest concern though.

"Can they track him?"

The president nodded. "Probably."

"Then why risk bringing him to one of your safe houses?"

"Besides that he's the reason you're here?" he said wryly, alluding to the fact that Armise was the reason I'd made it out of that stadium alive. "Doesn't matter if they can. None of us can really hide anymore."

I mirrored the president's posture, leaning forward in my chair. "Can I be sure?" I looked away, at the cross supposedly claiming my right as a son of a god I didn't believe in. "Can I be sure of him?" I clarified. "After the last twenty-four hours..."

The president nodded solemnly. "You should be asking that. Short answer is that none of us can know for sure. Especially if you—the man who is sleeping with him—are unsure. My personal opinion, however, after twelve years of contact with him, is that you can."

Twelve years. That confirmed Armise's assertion that he had been working for the States since before the DCR standoff.

I shifted in my chair. "You're the only one who's not shunning him. Do you trust him?"

The president shrugged, a casual gesture that few outside his inner circle would know he was capable of. "I trust him as much as I do Neveed."

"And me?"

The president shook his head and said with conviction, "There's no one I trust as much as you."

That the president's wife had once held that position was left unsaid. Sarai had been dead for well over a decade now. I knew the man in front of me still mourned her and that avenging her violent passing was one of the president's greatest motivations. Revenge had a way of eliciting a passionate, and often violent, response.

"The destruction of the stadium wasn't staged?"

"Merq," he chided me.

"Don't try, sir. It wouldn't be the first time you manufactured a mass genocide."

"Even I can't make it appear as if hundreds of thousands of citizens have been slaughtered and still keep them alive."

"I'm going to kill Ahriman for this."

"I know you will."

I'd earned his faith, and I wouldn't fail him. "So what does come next? What do you expect from Armise? From me?"

"Once you get your parents back, I'm going to need you to hunt all the Committee members down. All twelve of them and Ahriman. No survivors. The Opposition leadership needs to be scattered. You will have your opportunity for vengeance."

"Protocol limitations?"

There were treaties. Rules of war that had existed—if rarely followed—during active fighting of the Borders War. Chemsense had been a century ago but was still used. Reverbs held the same distinction. I had to know if I was constrained by any of those legal limitations.

"None," the president confirmed. "I don't assume that will be a problem for Armise either."

I crooked an eyebrow. "You're making him a Peacemaker?"

"That distinction no longer exists. You are both Revolutionaries now. The Continental States exist solely in name. I know Armise is used to working solo, but this will require the two of you to partner up, as it were. I need Simion and Jegs focused on other projects. Whether that means you actually hunt together or not will be your choice. I need them all dead. And we're talking within months, not years."

"When can I go after Ahriman?"

"I'll leave that to you. He can be first, last…I don't care either way. But you cannot allow your fury to cloud when and how it happens. Your orders are to wipe them all out as quickly as possible. I know you, Merq. You have singular focus, and eliminating Ahriman is a mission you cannot afford to get bogged down in. If you and Armise are able to develop a plan that attacks all of them simultaneously then do it. However, Ahriman's death can't be your only goal."

I had the overwhelming urge to tell the president to fuck off. Which meant that he was probably right. I frowned to show my displeasure but didn't comment on his orders. "Who's his second-in-command?" I asked instead.

"Chen is working on that."

I stared at him in disbelief. "How do we not know?"

"We're unclear on the exact power structure and how the Committee members and leaders within the Singaporean government fit into it, if at all."

"Which is why you need the clean slate."

"One reason, yes."

"Am I reporting to Neveed again?"

"You answer to me. His role as your handler has concluded."

At the very least that was one fewer complication in my life.

"When do you move?" I asked, remembering his intent to get to the front lines as soon as possible.

"A day or two. No more than that. Neveed will take up my residence in the capital at that point." The president tapped his fingers on the desk. "What's your end game, Merq?"

I huffed. "You ask that when I expected to die."

"And I know you already have it figured out."

"There is a...complication I'm in the process of integrating into my plans."

"Mm-hmm," the president muttered. "What is he to you?"

"I can't answer that," I replied honestly.

"You're so sure of yourself, Merq. And one man? This one man has the power to make you question your objectives."

I bit down on the piercing in my lip. "I don't pretend to understand it."

"And I don't have the power to change it," he said with finality.

I narrowed my eyes and sat back in the chair. A sickening awareness dawned inside me.

"He's a gift, isn't he?" I whispered.

"Don't be simple. That is perilously close to the flesh trade. That would be rather crass of me and quite inhuman."

"Of which you are neither," I said with a smile, and added, "sir."

The president laughed. "There are many who would beg to differ."

It wouldn't be long before every citizen understood the depth of President Kersch's commitment to an upending of the current geography and power structure of the world.

"And what is your end game, sir?"

"The same as it's always been. The balance of power returning to the people. Revolution is about life and unity. The value of the individual and the power of the collective. I've been a part of the wrong side of the movement for too many years now. It's going to be difficult to convince the citizenry that the vast majority of my actions were manufactured. The people have something to fight for, but we have to give them a compelling enough reason to lay down their lives—to threaten the peace of their homes and families once again—for that cause."

I scoffed. What was it with existential diatribes on fighting today? First Armise and now the president. Their apparent need to convince me of the rightness of our course of action was unnecessary and bordering on insulting. Especially when I knew that both of them held ulterior motives that stained the supposed purity of their intentions.

I scrubbed my hands through my hair and tried not to roll my eyes in response. "Fuck. Not you too."

"I suppose this distance you view the world with can be soundly laid at my feet and your upbringing. I wasn't wrong for setting you on this course, but that doesn't mean I was completely right either." The president waved his hands in the air as if he were gathering his thoughts. "You must be wondering why I led you to believe you were on that mission solo and would likely be killed when you assassinated the premiere. Or why I kept Armise's status as a Revolutionary operative guarded for as long as I did, especially when there is little that has ever been hidden between us. I personally would want to know."

I was surprised that he had decided to broach this topic with me. "Does the truth of his involvement really matter?"

"I can't possibly answer that for you."

I didn't have to think about my response. "I don't want to know. Rather, I don't need to know. You had your reasons and, more importantly, it's done."

"It's that easy for you?"

"Guess it is, sir."

He scratched at his chin and his features eased. "I've known you your entire life, Merq. Are you ever going to call me Wensen?"

I frowned. "No."

"You're my soldier, Merq, but I've come to think of you as more than that. I'd tell you that you are the son I never had, but I'm not in the mood to be laughed at. I have faith in you and your abilities. The Revolution is stronger because you are a part of it. And I have no doubt that every one of those Committee members' death dates is imminent. Ahriman's as well. I expect them all to suffer horribly, in recompense for every life taken tonight. You've always been effective. Detached but thorough. Armise brings a fire to you. I like the change."

At least one of us does.

"He complicates my work," I clarified for him.

"And clouds your head. I sympathize. Sarai did the same for me. At the same time, she was the only person in the world who could cut through it all. To know what I needed when I didn't. Sarai's protection of me was metaphorical, emotional more than physical, but real nonetheless. Armise will do for you as Sarai did for me and he will aid you in remaining alive. Don't discount the value of that type of partnership. Now, we need to talk about your parents."

My gut twisted at the abrupt change in conversation. "I'd rather talk about Armise."

"They don't deserve this callous dismissal."

"Yet they don't deserve my loyalty or life either."

The corner of the president's lips tipped into a smile. "But I do."

"True. When do you want me to move on them?"

"Do you even know what day today is?"

"Again I ask, does it matter?"

"Just an observation." The president activated his BC5 screen. "You move when I move. Exley is going to take you and Armise into the camps to scout the area in the morning—which, by the way, is in six hours. Impossible to tell time in this blackened hellhole. Have I told you how much I detest this bunker? Regardless, you and Armise will gather intel about the area where your parents are being held. But you don't move on any rescue until I've relocated. We have the jacquerie's support for now, so let's use that advantage. Chen has tracked the signatures of your parents' chips to an Opposition encampment on the outskirts of the capital, at the edges of the jacquerie camp. But I'm dubious to the reason why they remain in our territory at all. And there is a reason for it. Of that I have no doubt."

"Any intel on who's holding them?"

"Besides that they're Opposition? No."

"Where are you headed?" I prodded, knowing now was my sole opportunity to get information directly from him.

"The front lines in the DCR. Fighting is heaviest there, so I need to be on the ground."

"You need to not be killed," I insisted.

"We all die someday," he replied with a flippancy that aggravated me.

"By all means, sir. Your death will serve the Revolution well," I replied sarcastically. "Why am I even waiting for you to leave then?"

"I have a strong suspicion that Ahriman is using your parents as live bait."

"Because he knows of your history with them."

"Exactly. I want to believe I won't bend to emotional connections, but I won't risk it. Despite what you think, and what I say in jest, I have no intention of dying. I have responsibilities to fulfill. A Revolution to oversee, and perhaps see to its end."

"God willing." I sneered, showing just how much faith I had in any higher power being the one to save our asses.

"God willing, indeed," the president replied with sincerity. "Neveed will remain in the bunker until you've brought them in. Then they're to travel with him to my residence in the capital."

"They won't be expected to fight?"

"It's time we brought them back as faces for the Revolution. We will be exploiting your father's familial connection to the inventor of the sonicbullet. Their value is in front of the camera and with the press corps. Your career in broadcast ends here. As soon as you deliver them back here you and Armise are to start hunting the Committee members."

That was the mission I was prepared for. Looked forward to. I was at my best in a fight, whether undercover or with a team. Assassinations were also Armise's specialty, and I had no doubt that Armise would be eager to undertake the search for Committee members as well. I waited to see if he was going to add anything else, but when he didn't lift his eyes from his screen, I stood to leave.

"And Merq?" he called out, stopping me. "As usual, try not to die."

I ran my fingers through my hair and gave the president's guidance the one second of consideration it deserved. "I'll keep that in mind, sir."

He shook his head, smiling. "You do that."

The president leaned down over his screen and didn't make any further comment. I shut the heavy wooden door behind me and headed back toward my quarters.

The layout of the bunker was already feeling familiar. I took the branch off toward my quarters without encountering anyone else in the hallway as I walked. I slipped into the darkened room and back into bed, stripping only my shirt off before climbing under the sheet.

Armise stirred next to me, then turned over to face me. "What deadly and vicious agenda have you been asked to commit to now?"

"Us, not just me. We go tomorrow to scout the location where my parents are being held."

"When do we move on them?" It was a mirror of my question to the president. He was just as mission-oriented as I was.

"When the president vacates to the DCR."

"Is there anything else interesting that came up in your discussion?"

"Yeah." I sighed, remembering the president's comment that I needed to talk to Dr. Casas about Armise being genetmod. But I couldn't find the will to have this conversation now.

Armise stared me down. "Are you going to tell me? Or—"

"No way in hell," I interrupted him. "Not now."

Armise turned back over without a verbal reply, inching his body closer to mine. I threw an arm over his waist and burrowed my nose into the back of his neck. The chill coming off his skin began to wipe all thought away. Just how much knowledge Armise had of his own genetic modifications was a conversation I'd been holding off on for so long that there was no way one more night could make a difference.

The room was silent except for our breathing, the fighting up top still at a lull. Armise was in the bed next to me. I had six hours until my next mission commenced. And I couldn't remember the last time I'd known the length of time I was going to have off before I was called for duty again. I had six free hours. It had been years, if not decades, since I'd had this level of freedom.

I slipped my foot between Armise's calves and drew him closer.

I didn't know what I was doing or why. But it felt right. Human.

For once, I let the rest go.

Chapter Five

An alarm blared—screeched in my ears and ricocheted through my head—and I was awake, shooting up in the bed, grasping for awareness, trying to remember where I was. It didn't take me long—I was trained for quick response. I flung the sheets off and stalked to the closet, throwing the doors open and sorting through the hangers to find my uniform.

"We are not being attacked, what the fuck is the alarm for?" Armise's voice came from the bed.

I looked back at him. He hadn't moved from his relaxed position on his side of the mattress. Exactly where he'd been when I'd curled into him and fallen into a dreamless sleep.

The closet was filled with copies of the same all-black outfits with the sunburst symbol of the Revolution on the shoulder. I ran my fingertips over the emblem and snagged one of the sets off the hanger. I crossed the room and raised a BC5 screen on the desk. It was well after dawn and past the time the president had stated Armise and I would be called up to begin the scouting trip.

"How do you know we're not being attacked?" I asked incredulously as I flipped through status reports.

He gestured toward the ceiling but didn't move any farther. The alarm continued to blare. "No bombs. No gunshots or sonic pops. Or yelling. That is usually a good tell."

The alarm abruptly cut off, the sudden silence ringing in my ears.

"Fuck this," Armise ground out and yanked the covers over his head.

I pulled the uniform shirt on and shifted it into place, but it didn't fit as tightly as my uniform traditionally would. I pulled it off and looked at the tag. It was Armise's size, not mine.

I frowned and stalked back to the closet. A quick rummage through its contents revealed that the right side held uniforms in Armise's exact size and the left was lined with uniforms in my size—one step below Armise's massive width. I tried not to think about why the closet would have been stocked with clothes for both of us even though two rooms had supposedly been prepared for us. I knew it was likely the work of Neveed. Regardless of whether both rooms were stocked similarly—prepared with the idea in mind that Armise and I would be sharing a room instead of sleeping apart—it unnerved me that Neveed knew me well enough to anticipate this outcome.

It was neither welcoming nor helpful.

"I'm going to the control room," I said to Armise over my shoulder.

He grunted in response and sat up, wiping the sleep from his eyes. I smoothed down my uniform, tucked the shirt into the tightly fitting trousers and pulled on socks then my boots.

Armise leaned forward, putting his elbows on his knees and watching me with a predatory air.

I recognized that look immediately. But there wasn't time for any fucking around this morning, as much as my body protested the idea.

"You coming with me?" I asked, surprising myself that I bothered to ask the question.

"Yes," he huffed in response and got up from the bed.

"Right side," I directed him, cocking my head toward the closet.

"Same fucking side of the bed I sleep on," Armise murmured under his breath just loud enough for me to hear.

I hadn't considered it, but he was right. When had we become this predictable?

"Are there any reports coming through?" Armise asked as he dressed.

"Status reports are vague," I answered tersely, the need to be in action making me tense.

He glared at me. "What the fuck is your problem?"

"Besides that we're at war?"

"Good morning to you too," he replied with a sarcastic tone that sounded much more like me than him.

I didn't know how to answer his question. Yes, the alarm had been a shit way to be woken up. But there was nothing imminent as far as I could see from the status reports. I'd gotten a full night's sleep for the first time in years. The bombs weren't going off and I had a new mission. So why was I so uneasy?

It only took one look at the way Armise's uniform stretched across his powerful frame as he tugged it over his head to catch on to the obvious fucking conclusion.

I had spent the entire night with Armise in my bed. We hadn't fucked. I'd slept like the dead. I hadn't worried once about what would happen if we were discovered.

And I didn't know how to handle that.

Armise didn't turn when he said, "I am not in the mindset for your piss-ass mood. Take off. I will see you there."

Armise finished dressing and walked around the corner, shutting the door to the en suite.

I didn't wait for him.

I should have known exactly how to get back to the control room, but I took three wrong turns, relying on soldiers passing through the corridors to point me in the right direction. Before I approached the doors I took a deep breath and tried to clear my head of everything that didn't have to do with the Revolution or the mission to rescue my parents.

I walked into chaos.

The control room was jammed with soldiers and analysts scurrying around the enclosed area, sharing whispers over hunched groupings, then others blatantly screaming information across the small space. The air was stifling, hot, cramped, with the scent of sweat. And fear.

I searched the room and found Neveed huddled with Simion and Jegs. They parted, letting me into their cloistered group.

"What's going on?" I asked, keeping my voice pitched low.

Neveed surveyed my uniform with a twist of his lip before he answered. "Casualties are out of control."

"How many?"

"We're collecting intel now. It's in the thousands. The Opposition rallied much faster than we expected."

"As if they had some kind of a heads-up about what we were doing," I noted.

"Maybe. No way to know for sure."

"They sabotaged the shield stations in the DCR," Simion added.

"We're refocusing attacks on protecting the remaining power stations and battery stores," Neveed continued. "We have to maintain our advantage as long as we can."

"How are the artilleries holding up?" I asked.

"Still solid. We're prepared for the loss of shields on every continent."

"But?" I could hear there was something left unsaid by Neveed.

"They're going after transport stations too."

I caught on immediately. "We have to get the president out of here now before he's stranded."

"Already in process," Simion answered then he broke away from the group.

"What's our backup if the transports go down?" I asked.

"We've got a store of Thunders, but not many. Commercial airliners are grounded. We can take possession of any of them. But anything airborne will be a target. A targeted reverb will take them down without hesitation. I won't risk Kersch's life like that."

"What do you need from me?"

Neveed shook his head. "Your mission hasn't changed."

"No, Neveed," I challenged him. "No. I won't be focused on rescuing two people when the president is heading into an area where thousands of our fighters are being slaughtered." I threw Neveed's words back at him. "Where he is at risk."

Neveed stepped up to me. He was a head shorter than me, and couldn't match my bulk no matter how hard he worked out, but his position as the president's second-in-command was undeniable. "You have your orders."

I ground my teeth together in frustration. "How secure is the bunker?"

"Chen!" Neveed called out without turning to face her.

"Does it look like I have time to talk right now?" she yelled back.

"How long?" Neveed asked, refusing to cede any authority to her.

"They're breaking through our systems right now," she replied with a cool surety that sped my heartbeat.

"Any way to keep them out?" I asked her.

Chen cracked her neck and stared me down. "Nah, I'm just letting them through."

Neveed swore under his breath but didn't challenge Chen this time.

I felt a hand on my shoulder and found the president standing next to me, and Armise and Simion steadfastly stationed behind him to his left and right.

"Simion is trying to push me into the transport room," the president interjected. "Could I perhaps have a moment of your time to figure out why he's so insistent?"

I saw the rough grinding of Neveed's jaw before he answered. "The transport stations in the DCR are being attacked. This may be your only opportunity to get to the front lines."

"I'm not going anywhere. Not yet. I think they're trying to draw me there."

I scoffed. We were operating in a defensive instead of offensive mode. Did it really matter if my parents were being used as bait? Or if the president was being drawn to the DCR? He couldn't—and wouldn't—stay in this bunker forever. So we had to move him at some point.

And right now Neveed and the president were making tactical decisions based upon the actions of the Opposition. Reacting instead of decisively acting.

"You sure you're not just being paranoid?" I questioned the president, knowing that I was pushing the limits of how I should be communicating with him in front of his subordinates.

The president stared at me, unflinching. "I am being paranoid. It's the only way I've lived this long. Exley is ready to take you into the Underground." He motioned between Armise and me, the meaning clear.

"Sir—" I began.

"He'll meet you in the weapons room," the president said without hesitation and turned away from me while calling for Chen.

"I'm with you," Jegs said, a wary gaze flitting to Armise.

I rolled my shoulders, trying to dissipate some of my tension as I watched the president walk away. Then I turned my attention, and frustration, to Jegs. I didn't need her tagging along to make sure Armise didn't turn traitor on me. "If you're there for protection I don't need it."

"I'm only going part of the way with you. I have personal business to attend to."

I took in the determined set of her shoulders and from years of working with her just I knew where her personal mission was going to take her. "Jegs—" I started.

She held up her hand. "Don't. We all have our loose threads." She shot a glare at Armise. "I'm just tying mine off and cutting it loose."

"Fine," I answered, even though it was far from fine. I cocked my head in the direction of the door. "Let's go."

* * * *

Exley pushed the heavy metal door open, blinding me momentarily with the harsh rays of the midday sun. I slid on my glasses, shielding my eyes from the brightness. The air was hot, heavy and dry. It burned with each inhalation making me much more aware of my lungs than I wanted to be.

We hadn't brought any respirators with us—Exley had warned us that our standard-issue military gear was too conspicuous—but I worried about getting caught somewhere without access to the filters. Initial fighting in the capital had waned, contained to localized skirmishes. All our intel pointed to the Opposition rallying for an ambush on the city. I had to laugh at the analysts who considered it a surprise attack when we knew it was coming. I was more concerned about what was occurring that we didn't know about.

This mission fit soundly into that category.

I was sure there was someone within the president's inner circle who was feeding information to the Opposition—possibly directly to Ahriman. The sabotage of the shield stations and transports in the DCR could have been coincidence, strategy or merely a knee-jerk reaction to the sheer number of Revolution forces who had popped up on the continent, but I was inclined to believe it had more to do with the president's desire to be on the front lines. Just as we were seeking the elimination of the leaders of the Opposition, they would be planning the same for us.

We'd shed our uniforms before leaving the bunker, trading in the fitted black uniforms for the muted earth tones and humble cloth scraps of the jacquerie. While they weren't technically part of the Revolution, the citizen-led movement was an ally. For all intents and purposes, we followed the same agenda. But their leadership had long ago refused to cede what little power they did have to the vast machine that was the Revolution. So we worked in tandem—parallel lines—ideologies and actions that fought for a common future but never crossed.

Armise pulled at the sleeves of his tunic and grumbled.

I crooked an eyebrow in silent question.

"Too much fabric," he mumbled unhappily.

Exley and Jegs peered at him in disbelief.

"And you worried about the respirators being too obvious," I said.

The citizenry glanced at us suspiciously as we worked through the shops, past the water treatment plants and into the heart of the jacquerie camp—aptly named the Underground. The title wasn't indicative of their physical location but instead of the jacquerie's status as the poorest of the poor. The citizens forgotten, abandoned and used.

Regardless of how we dressed, our group was one that would be noticed wherever we went—Armise and I were heads taller, and Jegs had her fuck-it-all air that made people take an unconscious step back. Only Exley looked like he belonged. His plaited braids swung as he maneuvered us through a gated wall and into the tent city on the periphery of the capital. The guards stationed at the entrance watched us but didn't make a move to intercept us. They carried rifles—real ones, not sonic—belts filled with clips of those antiquated bullets.

"You armed them, too?" Armise asked as we passed by.

"Of course," Exley replied with a hint of annoyance. "We're allies to the Revolution."

"This is where I break off," Jegs interrupted, disappearing into the crowd.

"Do you know what that's about?" Armise inquired.

I looked to Exley first, who steadfastly pretended that he hadn't heard the question.

"Yeah." But I didn't explain further. If Jegs was truly cutting off her loose ends then there would be a major power shift coming in the war. But I didn't have much faith in her ability to definitively cut her ties. Jegs' brother was her emotional weakness.

Exley pointed down a line of ramshackle tents. "This way."

The sun was nearly relentless, only the battered wind-whipped structures providing safety from the dangerous rays. Plumes of gray dust kicked up and swirled around us as we moved deeper into the permanent encampment. The stench of sewage—ammonia, methane and fetid water—was overwhelming in spots. As was the pungent aroma of cheap mass-manufactured spices used to mask the complete inedibility of the food the citizens consumed. I crinkled my nose in distaste.

There were no children roaming the streets and I had to assume that that was a reaction to the instability that threatened them. We had to step over prone, weakened and diseased people sheltered under tarps. Had to dodge the determined press of citizens going about their daily business, their faces emotionless masks and with eyes like black voids that appeared too similar to Ahriman's for my comfort. Small animals skittered in the periphery of the aisles, sliding in and out of the intermittent shadows. The packed city was in perpetual motion, but nearly silent. I didn't know what kind of animal could exist in these conditions, let alone human beings.

Anger built within me at the injustice of it all. I hated that what I was witnessing was new to me. Shocking. I'd seen and participated in the atrocities of war, but I'd thought that there was no way any existence outside of those horrors could be worse. I was wrong. That I was this unaware of the harshness of their reality when it was in direct correlation with the cause I fought for was nothing less than unacceptable. Pathetic.

"How do they survive?" I managed to ask around the tightening in my chest.

"They don't," was Exley's stark answer.

"This is sick."

Armise stepped up next to me. "Where have you been, Merq? This is the life most of the citizenry leads worldwide."

His accusation cut way too close.

"Working," was my curt answer.

I'd never been into the tent cities. Never strayed far from the Peacemaker facilities in truth. I'd been in constant motion since actively taking on official missions. I didn't have a home of my own, preferring to use whatever barracks or beds were open as I came and went between the States and foreign soil. What I needed I carried with me or kept in the guarded military stores. My kit was usually ruined after each mission anyway. I didn't carry any remembrances of my life before. And except for the files I'd studied about my parents, I had no recollection of what they looked like. I couldn't have picked out their faces or voices if someone had had a gun to my head.

None of the other members of my team led the same life. Both Jegs and Simion had families and dwellings within the city, outside of military zones. The president had his official government residence as well as a string of safe houses throughout the country, along with his various bunkers, all partially designed with his feedback and tastes in mind. Even Neveed maintained the house he'd grown up in on the southern coast of the States.

I lived a disposable life. One disassociated from a cause I was tasked with protecting and advancing. It was a disconnect I'd never realized existed and that I couldn't find the justification for.

"How much farther?" I said, trying to force my thoughts back to our mission.

"We're cutting through the middle of the camp. There's an abandoned string of facilities on the other side of the Underground."

"Currently abandoned?" Armise asked.

"No one in the jacquerie will use them."

"Why?" I asked. "These people are resourceful. Why wouldn't they utilize permanent structures?"

"You'll see," Exley said with a glance in my direction.

I gritted my teeth and trudged forward, having to sidestep another prone form. "How close can we get?"

"They already know we're coming. Get as close as you want."

"You sure about that?"

"Which part? That they know we're coming? Yeah, I'm positive."

I huffed in frustration, sweat sliding down the back of my neck, making me uncomfortable despite the fact that I was wearing tattered clothes that flapped in the wind. "So why not come out in full uniforms and storm the place?"

It wasn't intended as a question, although I had framed it that way. My frustration at how inefficient this operation seemed was beginning to take over. For fuck's sake, we knew where my parents were located. The Opposition forces holding them knew we were looking for them and intended to mount a rescue. We were staring down our barrels at each other and yet we were toying with each other instead of just pulling the fucking trigger. Armise and I had been held back, delayed, and now were being ordered to gather intel for a mission that would be more useful as an outright attack.

"Because they're using our tracking chips against us. That part of our system has already been hacked. Chen can't keep them out—no matter how many times she kicks them out they find their way back in. May as well take our time and do this right."

"The president knows the systems have been compromised?"

"Yeah."

"So we're here because they're expecting us."

Exley shrugged. "I'm just your fucking escort."

I looked at Armise. He narrowed his eyes and flexed his jaw. He could feel it too. There was something else to this. Something both of us were missing and that the president hadn't shared with either of us.

"It's too quiet in the camp," I said, finally putting words to one of the aspects of this clusterfuck that was unsettling me.

"This isn't normal," Exley confirmed.

"I'm willing to bet it's not our presence here or the attacks."

"For it to be this pervasive? Yeah, it's something else."

"There aren't any kids," Armise said.

So he'd noticed it too.

"It's creepy," Exley said with a shudder.

This whole scenario wasn't feeling right. There were too many unknown variables, too many pieces not fitting together with the information we'd been provided. The president had been adamant about me rescuing my parents, but maybe the reason he'd put Armise and me on this mission was because there was more to it than just their return.

We passed through the last row of tents into a wide unoccupied area. As if it were a buffer zone between the Underground and what lay past its borders. There was an expanse of that fine gray dirt with no vegetation, then the crumbling remains of what I'd been told were former manufacturing facilities. But as soon they came into full view I knew better.

These were the former headquarters of the PsychHAgs.

"Is this where you were trained?" Exley asked in a quiet voice.

I stared at the building, trying not to remember any of those years, no matter if their training had made me a better soldier. I could only nod in response. I understood immediately why the jacquerie refused to occupy these buildings. If there was any truth to the notion that evil could exist as a physical thing, then this was the place it would manifest.

"We're done here," I instructed Exley. He nodded and led the way back through the tent city.

Armise looked over his shoulder at the deteriorating building. "We're being manipulated."

I gave him a clipped nod to acknowledge that I agreed with him.

We were definitely being manipulated.

But by who or what, I wasn't sure yet.

Chapter Six

The bombings restarted after we returned to the bunker.

The timing of them was farther apart than the initial barrage, but just like the first time, the ground shook beneath my feet with each blast. I felt the difference in distance from where they were striking based on the rolling of the ground. I wondered how long we could keep up this pace before we ran out of munitions. Before the citizenry went mad with the strain.

Before I went mad with the strain.

I stared at the ceiling, flat on my back on the mattress, and forced myself not to flinch, not to react when the room around me shook. I was alone in bed. Which was more normal than not. Armise could function on little to no sleep and the night before had been a rarity in our years together. With a start I realized it was the only night when I'd awoken before him. The first time I'd found him still in bed with me. The unease of his static presence wasn't gone, but definitely diminished after today—displaced with the surety that there were moving pieces that I had no knowledge of, but that were aware of me.

I was suspicious as to why the Opposition was holding my parents in the abandoned headquarters of the PsychHAgs. It was possible they'd chosen to utilize buildings on the periphery of the city—ones in which they would have a measure of control—but I doubted that any decision Ahriman made was coincidental. He'd told me just before my shot that he'd taken my parents for protection. I knew better—it was for insurance. A direct threat. What Ahriman hadn't anticipated or known was that I had no tie to them. The president was more my creator than they were.

That my parents were still alive despite my assassination of the Opposition leader was a complication. And his decision to hold them in the facility I'd nearly died in was in no way unplanned. Both the president and Neveed had to be aware of what the buildings were. Both were fully aware of the violent history the buildings represented. As well as my involvement in that time.

All of those facts, combined with the president's insistence that Armise and I were to lead this operation, were enough for me to conclude that the rescue of my parents was not the main purpose of that mission.

For some reason, that made the whole mission much more palatable.

There was no value in putting Armise's, my and our team's lives on the line for two people who hadn't been politically relevant in over three decades. Judged by the same standard, however, I didn't know if my legacy added up to much more.

Nothing I'd ever done had been enough. No mission, no death, had kept us from this inevitable point. We were no better off as a society than we had been when

I was tasked as a Peacemaker almost two decades ago and I didn't know if we would ever be.

Fatalism suddenly seemed much more reasonable.

I kicked my feet from under the sheets and tugged on a T-shirt and the loose cloth pants of the jacquerie. I left my feet bare and stole silently out of my room and through the hallways. It was the middle of the night and this wing was all residences, containing none of the operational rooms that would be active no matter the time of day.

It didn't take me long to hear the hushed sound of Armise's northern Singapore cadence coming from the galley, and I went to push open the door when I heard who he was speaking to.

"We live in a world of impermanence," the president said.

I stopped, my hand on the door, and waited to hear Armise's reply.

Armise didn't respond with the muffled snort of disbelief I would have expected from him. Instead I heard the scratch of chair legs against the floor, and a creak as if Armise was leaning forward in his chair and resting his elbows on the table in front of him. A table he apparently shared with the president.

"I don't know you, Armise," the president continued. "Not like I know him. But I can already tell that you two are very different people. Similar upbringings, nearly identical professions, but completely different outcomes."

"You have known him a long time."

"His entire life."

"You know him better than his parents do."

"Perhaps. We're all his family."

"*You* are his family," Armise insisted with a fierceness that surprised me. "Tell me, are they worth the risk of him dying to rescue them?"

"That's not for me to decide."

"Except that it is. You are the president. The commander of the Revolution. This is exactly your decision to make and denying that is tantamount to cowardice."

"No, Armise. I've asked enough of him. There will be more he can do. But this mission is important. One I owe to him whether he understands that or not."

"If he survives."

"He will. Merq doesn't fail."

There was silence for a moment then Armise said, "What aren't you telling us?"

But I didn't hear the president's answer. I was pulled away from the conversation when a hand rested on my shoulder in a gesture of familiarity. I stepped away from the door and turned to find Neveed, his body nearly pressed against mine, his breath a close, warm brush on my neck. Way too fucking close.

"How does it feel to hear yourself being psychoanalyzed?" He grinned as if he was amused by the notion.

I shrugged out of his grip. "Doesn't anybody fucking sleep in this place?"

I elbowed the door open. If Armise and the president had been talking about things they didn't want me to hear then the guilt of it didn't register on either of their faces. As if it would anyway. They were both too practiced at deceit to give much away in their expressions.

I chose the chair at the head of the table, Armise to my left and the president to my right. Neveed followed me inside, moving to stand behind the president and lean against the wall. Armise was in a training uniform, having disposed of his jacquerie outfit as soon as we got back to the bunker. His black tattoos snaked from under the sleeves of his T-shirt. The sunburst emblem of the Revolution stood out against the black fabric and I had to wonder if he thought anything of wearing an insignia that identified him as something other than the Singaporean he'd been his entire life, or if this was just another piece of cloth, a meaningless decoration.

"Armise tells me you plan on moving on with the rescue as we discussed," the president said.

I sat back and crossed my arms. "There's no reason to rush unless you give me intel that says otherwise. Has there been a change to your plans?"

Neveed glanced at Armise. Apparently his personal distaste for Armise hadn't lessened despite him coming through on my rescue. "We haven't made that decision yet," he answered for the president.

"You're lying," I said. He was evading the subject because of Armise's presence in the room.

"This is not the place for this discussion."

The president didn't interject, leaving Neveed and I to re-establish the boundaries between us. Neveed was his second-in-command and up until two days ago had been my handler. He wasn't anymore though. As a newly minted general he outranked me, but from the president's own admission he trusted me more than Neveed.

I had no issues with speaking my mind in front of any of them. It occurred to me that that might have been because, out of all of them, I had the least to hide. There was already too much unsaid between us—all of us—for me to bother with civility or a standard of decorum that didn't apply to the fucked-up tangle of relationship issues filling the room. At least I'd never slept with the president.

"You won't talk about it because Armise is here."

"Correct," Neveed answered.

Armise gave a low chuckle and got up from his seat. "I will leave you to it."

I grabbed Armise's wrist, stopping him. From the corner of my eye I could see him look down at me, but I didn't break eye contact with Neveed. "Wait up for me."

Neveed's nostrils flared with disgust.

Armise nodded and was gone, the door clicking shut behind him.

"I leave tomorrow," the president answered when we were alone.

"For the DCR?"

He nodded. "It's where I need to be."

"And I need to be here." I didn't bother to hide my disdain for the idea in my tone.

The president tapped his fingers on the table. "For now."

I wanted the information Armise had been seeking before I walked in. "What aren't you telling us?"

"You know I won't answer that."

"I had to ask." I pushed back from the table in frustration. "Goodnight."

I was still seething when I opened the door to my quarters.

From the en suite there was the sound of running water and the door was open, light spilling into the otherwise dark room. Armise was positioned in front of the mirror, slathering one of his balms over his chin, using the fragrant, foreign mixture to ease the glide of steel over skin. I leaned against the jamb and watched him. The knife in his right hand elicited a rough scratching noise as he pulled it down his cheek, the silver and black hairs of his beard falling into the sink.

"He leaves tomorrow," I offered.

"He told me that earlier."

"You two have fun catching up?"

Armise eyed me in the mirror. "Jealousy suits Neveed much better than it does you."

I flinched, but continued on. "What was his answer to you on what he's hiding from us?"

"That it was my choice to be here."

I opened my mouth to say one thing, then went with my first thought. "Is it still your choice?"

Armise drove the tip of the knife into the polymaterial counter. "What the fuck does that mean?"

"You don't have anywhere else to go."

Armise glared at me. "Neither do you."

His assertion was true enough, but it wasn't what I wanted to hear. I decided to change tactics.

"The president said I don't fail. Yesterday he told me that he trusts me above anyone else. I don't know if that trust is earned or by default."

Armise laid his palms on the counter, maintaining eye contact through the mirror. "That matters to you."

I didn't think it would. But… I nodded in reply. "It does."

Armise gripped the handle of the knife and yanked it free. He flipped it, caught it by the blade and handed it to me. "I haven't done anything except trim this beard in nearly twenty years. I want it gone."

I plucked the knife from his hand. "Why now?"

Armise's eyes locked on to mine. "My trust has been earned."

I approached him slowly and gripped his chin, tipping his face to the side. The coldness of his skin lit every nerve in my hand until a chill was running in waves up my arms. I pressed my body against his and placed the blade to his neck. Skin, muscle and sinew dipped under the pressure of the ancient steel Armise maintained with lethal sharpness. It would have been easy to slice through his neck. A strike that would be quick, fatal and nearly painless. But I didn't. And Armise knew I wouldn't.

The last two days had been a lifetime's worth of change. Of shifting perceptions, with more questions than answers.

Knowing full well that I was delving into the topic I'd avoided for years now, I asked, "What's your core temperature?"

He swallowed, the motion lifting the knife by a fraction as I dragged it down his skin.

"It fluctuates with my surroundings. Anywhere from eighty-eight degrees to one-hundred-eight."

I took that information in, and tried to reconcile it with what I knew about normal human anatomy. At the lowest end of that spectrum he should have been comatose—at the highest his blood would be close to boiling.

"How much did they modify?"

Armise's lip tipped up. "I don't know."

I searched his eyes. "What are you hiding?"

"What are you hiding, Merq?"

I didn't have to hesitate. "Nothing."

"I would not make that declaration too quickly."

"I'm not the president or Neveed. I am a cog in the machine, not a designer."

Armise tipped his head back, exposing his neck further to the blade so I could get to the hair under his chin. "You are the piece that when left on the table people are clueless as to why the machine no longer operates as smoothly as it should."

I stopped with the knife inches from his neck.

He flicked the underside of the blade. "Go ahead, take it all off."

"Why?"

"Which question? You tend to ask a lot of them."

I shrugged. "Pick one."

Armise inhaled. "I do not want to be anywhere else."

"Okay." I smoothed more balm over his skin then pressed the blade to his cheek. I made the conscious decision to believe him.

"Tell me about the building where they are holding your parents," he said.

"They're the former headquarters of the PsychHAgs—psychological health agents."

"I know of it. Fucked-up program. I have heard they do not operate anymore."

"Not officially," I confirmed. "That campus has been vacant for as long as you've had this beard. They shut down that particular facility after my training class. I was the only one to survive."

Armise's silver-blue eyes took in my features, pierced me. "This rescue… It is not solely about your parents."

I dragged the knife blade along the line of his jaw. "I know."

"Any idea what it is really about?"

I drew the knife away and met his gaze. "If I did, I would feel a lot less powerless."

It was an admission that shocked me as soon as I said it. There had been major aspects of my missions that I'd never been briefed on. Moving pieces my superiors analyzed and used me to manipulate. But I'd always been aware of what the end game was. The president was giving me a vague call to the Revolution as my guiding principle and revenge as a motivation. I had no doubt, despite his assertion I needed to remain calm and focused, that he was attempting to steer me into anger. Because he, more than anyone else, understood that my desire to kill Ahriman and all the Committee members had the potential to blind me to the parts he didn't want or need me to see. Normally, his tactics would have worked.

One simple act by Armise had changed all of that. His defection from Singapore to be at my side had shifted how I viewed everything around me. Maybe that was a part of the unease I couldn't seem to shake. I'd never let anyone get close enough to me to have that much of an impact on my life.

I scraped away the black and silver hairs on Armise's face, cut down to the skin, exposing scars long hidden beneath the scruff. Slices of white across his angular features. Armise closed his eyes and set his body against mine—one of his hands on the counter, the other gripping my hip. I worked slowly down his cheeks, under the defined line of his jaw and around the curve of his lips. Armise breathed steadily, his chest rising and falling, pressing against mine.

When I'd scratched off the last of the hairs I stepped back and ran the knife under the running water, wiped it dry on my shirt and offered the blade back to him.

Armise gripped the handle of the blade and I let go. He slid it into the sheath.

Armise ran his fingers over his cheek and down his jaw, his thumb coasting over his bottom lip. "You're only powerless if you let them take away your power. And you are stronger than any of them."

I didn't buy that at all.

"Even you?"

Without warning Armise spun on me, barreling into my chest, lifting me off my feet and slamming me to the floor. I couldn't stop the fall—his momentum was too great, his ability to anticipate my defensive reactions and leverage my weaknesses too practiced—but I was fast enough to swipe his knife from the sheath on his hip. As we fell I slipped his blade out. When we came to a rest Armise's body covered mine, pinning me to the floor, and I held his own weapon with white knuckles to his throat, the length of the blade drawing a thin line of blood across his neck.

Armise didn't even flinch.

"You will never be stronger than I am, Merq," Armise stated, the movement of his throat causing the blade to cut in farther. I eased the steel just a fraction away from his skin. He pressed his neck into the blade until his lips were nearly on mine—with each fraction of movement I was forced to either move the knife with him or to deepen the mark where his blood beaded. I relented, letting the steel fall away from his neck, but I spun the handle and gripped it in my fist.

Armise dipped his head down and rubbed his freshly shaven cheek over my lips and along my jaw. The smoothness was new, his scent familiar, the desire now thrumming through me unavoidable.

"But," he whispered against my skin, "that is why I am here. We fight together and the world has no choice but to drop to their knees and beg for mercy."

I arched into him and inhaled the fading scent of Singaporean balms, of him. I bit at his earlobe and scratched my jaw along his. "Mercy which neither of us is likely to give."

Armise dragged his lips across my neck and down to my collarbone and nipped at the fabric of my T-shirt. "Put the knife down, Merq," he urged. His hands tugged at the hem of my shirt. "And take this off."

I wrapped my arm around his shoulders, his muscles shifting subtly at my touch. I put the edge of the blade at the base of his neck under his shirt and sliced through the black fabric. "You first."

Armise rubbed his torso against mine then sat up, straddling my hips. He ripped the remains of his shirt off, his hips rolling with the movement, pressing our thickening lengths together.

I released the knife, sent it skittering across the floor, and in a rush sat up and removed my shirt, then kissed him deeply. Desperately. I had gone much longer periods of time without touching Armise, without him making me come, but I'd never had him in this close proximity for an extended amount of time and not fucked him. I needed. There was no other word for it.

My skin was alight with that fevered, aching desire only he could extinguish—that blissful, deceptive heat of drowning in icy water. My brain registered warmth even as his cold enveloped me, pulling me under. I shivered and burned at the same time, fought for breath and inhaled his scent more deeply. I savored the insistent, painful press of his cock against mine, still too clothed for the friction to be enough.

Armise pushed at my waistband and gripped my dick in a firm fist. I pumped into his hand. Licked at his lips. Put my hand behind his neck and forced our bodies closer together, his tongue snaking into my mouth. We kissed wildly—with Armise there was no other way. Rushed, grasping on to each other with frantic need. As always the real world fell away and all I could think about was this man and the unrelenting pace he silently commanded of me. He rocked against me, driving his tongue deeper into me then drawing back and teasing at my lip piercing. His hand worked me rapidly to the edge while his other arm wrapped around my ribs and clutched my back, forcing me to arch into his chest. I could feel his heart thudding, speeding, my own quickening in response.

I broke away from the kiss, gasping for breath. "Off. Everything. Now," I ordered.

His silver eyes went black, the pupils swallowing the shifting irises. Armise stood, dropped his pants to the floor and swiped the balm off the counter. I stripped off my pants and stroked myself. Armise tossed the container down to me and I slathered my cock. He dropped to his knees, straddling my hips. I gripped the base of my cock and teased the tip against his hole, lubing him, already beginning to drive inside him. Armise eased himself onto my dick, taking me deeper with each roll of his hips.

His movement was slow, torturous, and I tried to slam into him, but he gave a wicked grin and lifted himself off me every time I tried to force my way inside.

"Fucking now," I ground out, dragging my lip piercing between my teeth. I pushed at his shoulders but his knees were locked, keeping him hovered above me. He put his hands behind him and gripped my thighs in a painful grasp. I hissed and wrapped my arms around his, yanking his wrists together and into an iron grip. I lifted my hips and thrust inside him. Armise threw his head back and pushed back against me, driving me deeper. I could no longer feel the cold—only fire remained as he rode me, using his powerful thighs to lift himself then slam down on my aching cock.

I kissed his neck, curled my face into the curve of his shoulder and let him take over. His dick rubbed against the ridges of my stomach and while that would never have been enough for me, for Armise I knew it would be. Even though I held his hands back, Armise controlled the pace, riding me harshly, his tight heat dragging me under, his sweat-slick chest sliding against mine. He increased his pace, arched his back and buried my cock in his ass to the hilt, his body shaking, releasing, his hot cum spilling over my stomach. I thrust into him, the waves of his release tightening his hole and ripping the orgasm from me.

I let go of his wrists and collapsed to the floor, the weight of Armise an unwelcome pressure on my overly sensitive skin. I slapped at his ribs, urging him to get off me, and he obeyed with a huff, ending up in a sitting position against the wall. I threw an arm over my eyes and listened to my heartbeat, still thundering in my ears.

His words from earlier intruded into my consciousness.

'I don't want to be anywhere else.'

My eyes snapped open.

Maybe I was wrong. Maybe it wasn't that Armise and I had nowhere else to go.

Maybe this—us—was the only stability either of us had anymore. And I could be okay with that or I could fight it. Embrace it or shut him out. He was leaving the decision up to me.

I heard Armise get up and start the shower, the humid heat of the water billowing out in clouds around him.

"Come on, Merq," he coaxed me with an outstretched hand. "Shower then sleep."

I took his hand and allowed him to lift me from the floor. I clutched his hand, held onto it a beat longer than I normally would have and waited for that familiar unease to spread through me. But nothing came.

"Okay," I responded and stepped under the spray, Armise climbing in behind me.

Okay, I repeated in my head.

Maybe if I repeated that enough times it actually would be.

Chapter Seven

"Come on, Chen. You have to give me something on this," I hissed at her in a whisper. I peered over my shoulder to make sure there was no one in the packed control room who could overhear us.

"You want this one to be your freebie?"

"Just when I begin to forget you're a child."

She stuck her tongue out at me. "You sure about your strategy here?"

"One thing," I begged, holding up a single finger. "I don't need all the intel and details. Just a hint of what I'm walking into. You owe me."

"That is a mutual debt."

I waited.

"Fine," she relented. "I'm picking up a third signal from the building. A tracking chip that's definitely Revolutionary in origin."

"So the Opposition is holding someone else."

"Definitely. But I'm not sure who it is. This signal is an old chip. At least a decade, maybe more. And I can't find any matches to it in the database."

I sat back. Anyone who was active with the Revolution would have had their chips updated numerous times in the last ten years. "You think this person is important?"

She shrugged. "I'm not the one making that call."

It definitely wouldn't have been her making that decision. It would have to be either Neveed or the president giving her the command to keep this third person a secret. Regardless of who was giving the order, the presence of a third person, an associate of the Revolution in some way, was something I should have been informed about. That I wasn't being provided that detail, that I wasn't being ordered to extract this person as well, meant that whoever was giving the order was unsure about whether this unknown person was viable for the cause anymore. At least I now had confirmation that my instincts about this mission had been on.

I clapped her on the back in appreciation as Simion approached her then stood.

"I see you and Armise are ready," Neveed observed as he came up next to me, taking in my Revolution uniform.

I pointed across the control room and made sure to speak up above the clamor when I said, "Exley is coming with us too."

The room went silent. Analysts' heads popping above their computer screens, Simion freezing in mid-conversation next to Chen.

"Fuck, no." Exley shook his head adamantly, his braids swinging. "Nope. No. I'm not walking into a trap. They know you're coming."

"They can't track our systems," Chen replied, not taking her eyes off the screens in front of her. The lie slipped through her lips without hesitation.

"Bullshit," I spat out. "That lie is a waste of breath. It doesn't matter that they have access to our systems though. They won't see us coming."

Chen spared me a glance, her eyebrow lifted.

"My tracker chip is coming out."

"What?" Chen and Simion said at the same time.

"The transport and communication chips as well. I want them all removed." I laid my palms on Chen's desk and stared her down, ignoring Simion. "Everything."

"Everything?" Simion's voice came from the other side of Chen. By his tone he was questioning the possibility there would be more than the standard three every soldier had implanted in their wrists.

"Even the ones I don't know about," I insisted.

"I don't know what you're talking about," Chen said. She was lying. Again.

I had to give credit to Chen. She was young but had the coolness of decades of deceit. I had no proof there were more, but I was going with my intuition on this one. I was a high-value asset. The Revolution had spent years training me, and the president counted on me to accomplish the impossible. I wasn't fool enough to think that they wouldn't be protecting their investment with additional monitoring. As sure as I was that Armise was genetmod, I had to wonder how much of my own DNA had been played with. The possibilities of what they could have inside me were endless.

"I'll say this one more time. Even the ones I don't know about. I want them all out."

"Me too." Armise's voice came from behind me.

My head snapped around to face Armise. He'd known I was going to demand the removal of my chips, but hadn't said anything about removing his own. The thought of him being as untrackable as me made me nervous, and I wasn't sure why.

"We won't be able to transport you out if you get into trouble," Simion said.

I kept quiet. Held my ground.

Neveed stepped into our conversation. "Do it."

Chen glared at him. "You don't have the authority to order that."

"He does," the president interjected, appearing at my side. Dr. Feliu Casas, the head doctor for the president and the Revolution, stood behind him. The president spoke over his shoulder to Feliu. "Take the chips out of Merq and Armise. All of them."

"All? You sure about that?" Chen asked again. Beneath her stony exterior there was the faintest of tells—a twitch to her fingers where they hovered over her screen. She was just as nervous about the prospect of having me untrackable as I was about Armise.

"Put him under for it," the president instructed to Feliu. Then he put his full attention back on me. "I need you to trust me on this."

I nodded in agreement. Despite the president keeping me in the dark about certain aspects of this mission, I could trust him. He'd hidden information from me, but never without reason, and never in any way to violate the trust I put in him. I didn't know what they were removing from my body, why it had been put there in the first place or why I would need to be sedated to have it removed. Was it the location of the chips? Or that they didn't want me to see what they were pulling out of me? But if that was the way the president wanted it then I wouldn't fight him on it.

"Exley's too," the president added.

Exley put his head in his hands and huffed out a long breath, seemingly resigning himself to the fact that he would be going with us whether he wanted to or not.

"Shit. Fine," he conceded.

"There's no guarantee with the Singaporean," Chen pointed out. "We don't know what he's carrying."

"Then I'll remove the obvious ones," Feliu replied, joining our already too-crowded discussion.

"So it's just going to be the three of you on this op?" Simion asked.

"Yeah."

I didn't offer any other information on what Armise and I had planned. Simion didn't need to know. None of them did. Armise and I were going to have to use unconventional tactics for this mission. Making sure they couldn't track us wasn't just to evade the Opposition. And Exley's participation wasn't just to get us through the Underground without a hassle.

I looked around the room, scanning the faces.

"Where is Jegs?" I asked.

Neveed crossed his arms and frowned. "She hasn't come back yet."

That wasn't a positive development. Hopefully she was tying those loose ends up definitively enough that her personal issues wouldn't impact what we were trying to do.

I mirrored Neveed's pose, drawing myself up to my full height. "How long are we going to leave her out there?"

"She's on her own with this one, Colonel."

"Agreed. But if we get any intel that her side job is fucking up our long-term agenda then we need to pull her back in. Regardless of whether or not her business is concluded."

Chen looked to the president for verification of this directive. He nodded in agreement. She lifted another screen from her desk and typed in a series of commands. Apparently whatever method they used to monitor us was something that Chen oversaw and possibly controlled.

Simion handed me a box. "Take this. It's an in-ear. Old technology using radio waves. If we can't communicate through the chip this will be your last-ditch way to reach us."

I opened the box, surveying the heavy black plastic pack with a thin black cord connected to it and a circle on the end that was just the right size to fit into my ear. "Infochip discovery?"

"Something like that," Chen murmured.

I frowned again, took the device out of the box, snapped it closed and handed it back to Simion. "Let's get this over with."

* * * *

"You want surge to combat any post-op pain?" Feliu asked as he bent over my body, slipping an IV port into my vein.

We were in a procedure room much like the one I'd been placed in to recover after the DCR standoff. Armise and Exley had been taken to other rooms, the three of us splitting off into separate directions as we'd left the control room.

"No. I need to be clearheaded. And I don't intend on getting injured."

"Stubborn and stupid," Feliu chided me.

I couldn't argue with him on that point.

Feliu took the needle in hand and went to inject the sedative. I put my hand over his, stopping him.

"I need the room cleared first."

Although it had appeared as if the medical staff was ignoring our conversation, they vacated the room immediately with my request.

When the door clicked shut behind them, I asked the question the president had suggested I delve into with the doctor. "How genetmod is he?"

Feliu took a step back and slid a stool to the side of the bed, sitting down before he answered. "The president told you."

"Just answer me."

"Armise's base DNA is heavily modified. There appears to be forced improvements to the genes controlling strength, sight, hearing and touch. His body temp when he transported into the bunker was just over ninety degrees. I thought I was going to have to treat him until all his other vitals came back normal."

"He told me his temperature fluctuates to match his surroundings."

"It's an impressive modification. Our scientists haven't figured out how to do that."

There was nothing the doctor had told me yet that surprised me. Armise had already admitted as much to me. And all the changes Feliu mentioned would be necessary to improve Armise's sniper ability. But there had to be something else if the president was bringing it to my attention.

"What else?"

"I would have assumed to also see rapid healing but that seems to be missing. It's a mod we're only starting to master, so maybe they're just not there yet."

I heard more of what the doctor wasn't telling me than what he was. "Fuck, doc. But?"

"Singapore may have found a way to shield without a chip. And for protecting something other than sonicbullets."

I scowled. "What the hell does that mean?"

"That's just it. I don't know. We can read a whole lot about him, but I don't trust the data. There's a glitch. A blip. Something inside him we can't see and is being actively hidden from us."

"How do you know that?"

"Part intuition, part experience. I've done a lot of scans. His vitals take a moment to register. The mechanical hesitation is so fast it could be written off to equipment fluctuations, but I…I think it's more."

"They're shielding something inside him," I said.

Feliu nodded thoughtfully. "Or allowing through only the information they want us to see."

Fuck. That Singapore may have had the ability to use modifications to hide information from us was potentially disastrous. Who was I kidding, though? Neither option was optimal.

"You think he knows what it is?" Feliu asked.

I shook my head. "No."

"You seem sure about that."

I settled my head back and extended my arm to him. "Part intuition, part experience. Let's get this over with."

Chapter Eight

We couldn't breathe without respirators. Another electrical storm had passed through the capital last night and that, in combination with the stench of ignited gunpowder and dust off the kicked-up, bombed-out streets, left the air less than hospitable. Thin on oxygen and weighted with particulates. The masks over our mouths and goggles used to protect our eyes would also have helped to hide our identities, if we had at all been concerned about that.

We were dressed in our Revolution uniforms, not bothering with the jacquerie getups this time around. Yes, I was hoping that removing our chips would keep them from immediately tracking us, but I knew that wasn't likely. Even if they couldn't track Exley or me, we didn't know what tracking systems existed within Armise besides the normal chips.

I'd used the Opposition hack into our systems as an excuse more than anything else. I'd wanted my chips out of me—perhaps permanently—and this mission had provided the best cover for that request.

I trusted the president, but he was the only one in that control room besides Armise whom I trusted. The rest of them could fuck off. Armise was the only one I cared about knowing where I was, and for the foreseeable future we wouldn't be far from each other, so why did I need any of my chips?

My step was lighter knowing they weren't there anymore, my thoughts and intentions clearer without the burden of their prying presence. It was the first time since I was sixteen that some kind of tracker wasn't keeping me tethered to command. If the president was good on his word that they had removed everything, I was operating outside of the system—even more so than normal.

There were few who had the power or the money to opt out of the validated identification system mandated by every government. Children were implanted with trackers at birth. The optional chips were highly coveted—despite the knowledge that every time a chip was used it was monitored—and they cost way more than the vast majority of citizens could afford. Communication chips were rare and transport ones even more so. Every citizen was tracked, their movements stored in servers scattered across the globe, each government collecting various bits of information, all with the purpose of controlling their individual agendas.

I'd run into very few people who were able to make it completely off grid. Most of them were soldiers for hire, deviants or criminals, utilizing the technology to manipulate the system and mask their true intentions.

That there was someone being held by the Opposition who had evaded notice for this long was troubling to me. Criminals knew how to run the black market and trade out or manufacture chips that disguised their identity. But I'd never heard of anyone maintaining old technology. Old trackers, even the decommissioned ones, were still logged in to the system so they could be tied to one citizen. That this person didn't exist in any of the databases brought a host of questions. None of which I would have the answer to until we found out who he was.

It was yet another complication. And I really didn't like complications.

Armise kept point at my right shoulder, scanning the weather-beaten tent city. He carried his rifle across his chest, ready to fire. Exley had a pistol at his hip, but I wasn't sure if he even knew how to use it.

I had over-prepared, bringing a rifle, two pistols that sat at my hips, and knives strategically placed over my body. Neveed had even pushed a grenade into my hand at the last minute, saying that you never knew what might be needed.

The Opposition forces remaining in the city were scattered. Fighting had been heavy over the last four days, and the Revolutionaries were hunting them down and killing them en masse. The bombs were taking out the Opposition gatherings we could detect. All the transport centers across the city were now held by Revolution forces, so we didn't worry about Opposition forces sneaking in that way.

We weren't to the point in the war where Opposition forces could bribe their way into militarized zones. That would come later, when the hardcore Revolutionaries were worn down and desperate, unwilling to put the cause above their own survival. Hopefully we'd never get to that point.

In front of me, Exley surveyed the area then dropped into step with me.

"You ready to tell me the real reason I'm here with you?"

I considered lying to him. Then didn't. "Because you know what my parents look like."

Exley tripped over his feet, caught himself with a hand to my arm that made me more twitchy. I kept walking.

Exley eyes widened as he put together the pieces of why I needed him on this op. "Shit. You've only seen the files."

"We have to be sure it's them," Armise added.

Exley nodded. "Yeah, no problem. I got this."

"You know how to use that thing?"

Exley looked at the device in his hands that Chen had given him to monitor the tracking chips in the vicinity. "I've used one before. This is more advanced, but technology and I are on good terms."

"I meant the gun."

Exley pursed his lips and shook his head.

Well, wasn't that just fucking great. That was now four people Armise and I would have to protect from an unknown number of Opposition forces. Plus get ourselves out alive.

More complications. I ground my teeth together.

"So what's up with the shave?" Exley asked, his gaze swiveling over the empty camp.

It took me a moment to center in on what he was asking, then I turned toward Armise, barely restraining a smile. I crooked an eyebrow and Armise huffed.

"It was time for a change," Armise grumbled in reply.

Exley fidgeted with the device in his hands. "What's that myth you've told me about, Merq? The one about the guy who cut off all his hair and lost his power?"

I didn't bother to correct him on the origins of the story. That it was from the Christian Bible and not in fact myth. But it wouldn't have mattered. Exley had sat in on enough of my history lessons with Chen to make conversation, but still be embarrassingly uninformed.

"Samson," I said with a smile.

"Yeah, that's the one. You don't see my shearing off these braids. I'm not risking it."

"Well maybe if your dry-ass country was not so barren my skin wouldn't be this itchy," Armise quipped.

"Singapore's only one transport away," Exley retorted, then swore out loud when the device in his hands beeped, indicating the presence of someone new in the area.

Armise and I acted without thought, scrambling for cover, ducking under the tattered tarp of a citizen's home. Armise and I made sure the makeshift structure was empty before facing the alley again as Exley slipped in behind us.

"What is it, Ex?" I whispered, scanning the tents around us for movement.

"We've got incoming. One person. Just transported in."

"Where'd they come in from?"

"Don't know. It's a split sequence. Designed to mask the origination mark."

"Anywhere around us?"

Exley studied the device for another heartbeat. "In the building. Not in the camp."

"And you're sure the three signals we're tracking are still there?"

"It's still clocking back to them," Exley verified.

I stepped up to Armise, keeping my rifle trained on the alley even though Exley had said the new arrival wasn't around us.

"What are you thinking?" I whispered to him. "A lure? Bait?"

Armise knew without me telling him that I was talking about the real reason for my parents being held in this location.

"Bribe," Armise said definitively.

I searched his face, taking in the set of his jaw and the way his entire demeanor became more guarded, his attention laser-focused when he was in full-tilt battle mode. And there was only one reason he would make that swift a change.

"You think he's here."

"Who?" Exley asked, his voice cracking with fear.

Armise nodded, confirming that we were thinking the same thing.

"Ahriman Blanc," I replied over my shoulder.

Exley rotated on his heel to retreat but I grabbed his arm, yanking him back.

"No fucking way!" he began and I shot him a look to keep his voice down. He waved his hands in the air and whispered emphatically, "I did not agree to anything that has to do with him."

I'd never seen Exley frightened, but I supposed if anyone deserved that reaction it was Ahriman. Then Exley pulled his pistol and aimed it at me.

I eyed him. "Don't fucking point something at me you don't know how to use."

Armise yanked the weapon out of Exley's hand. "Or at least take the safety off."

Exley turned on Armise and grabbed for the gun, which Armise kept away from him. "What the fuck is a safety?"

"Fucking ancient technology." I motioned for Armise to give the gun back to Exley.

Exley palmed the weapon, his brow furrowed as he appeared to be trying to piece together what part of the hunk of metal in his hand was the safety.

I sighed and flipped the lever down. "This is the safety. You have to release it to fire. Only once then it will be ready. You want it off or on?"

"I'm going to shoot myself. Leave it on."

I flipped the lever back into place and he put the gun into his holster. Exley picked up the tracking device where he'd dropped it into the gray dust during his attempt to run.

"How many other people are you registering on that thing?" I asked.

Exley cracked his neck and I could see him trying to get himself back under control. "Your parents, the new arrival and the mysterious nomad. That's it."

"No one else?"

Exley flashed me an annoyed look. "What did I just fucking say?"

Armise ignored him and spoke to me. "There could be more soldiers in the building if their chips were removed. Or they could be using some kind of shield?"

I drew my rifle across my chest. "No. It's only them and him."

I was certain now that Ahriman was leading us into some kind of a trap.

"We go without the masks," I ordered and ripped mine off, discarding it on the ground and listening to Exley's mumbled protests as he got rid of his too.

I stepped out of the enclosure into the sunlight and defiantly continued toward the PsychHAg buildings. Armise was in step with me immediately and I heard Exley scrambling behind us to catch up.

"You're just going in?" Exley said with disbelief.

"That's the plan," I answered.

"That was not the plan," he insisted. "Not even close to it."

"It is now."

We crossed over the barrier between the tent city and the buildings, the nervous energy nearly rolling off Exley as he took up a shielded position behind Armise and me.

Before I pushed through the door of the main PsychHAg building, I had to consciously wipe away the memories that came flooding back. The lingering trauma from those days couldn't set me off my intent. I wouldn't allow it.

The building itself was in near-pristine condition when we entered. No longer furnished, and covered in a layer of the same gray dust that floated around the Underground, but unlike some of the other abandoned buildings I'd had the privilege to hole up in over the years, this one hadn't been ransacked or picked apart for usable materials. The entryway was as I remembered it. Military-grade polymaterials in the windows, metal archways and stark white walls.

"They're to the south. Upstairs," Exley said, looking at the tracking device. "Possibly in two separate rooms."

"Which floor?"

"Third."

Of fucking course they were.

I knew exactly where we were headed. The 'practice rooms' as the PsychHAgs had so delicately called them. And I had no doubt I would find Ahriman and my parents in the room my bloodied, half-dead body had been carried out of on the day the program was shut down.

We had three flights of stairs to go up to get to that half-level above the floor of classrooms. With Exley's ragged breaths and the nearly deafening thuds of his boots as he tromped across the dusty floor, Ahriman would hear us coming. It didn't matter, he already knew I was here. I shouldered my rifle and approached the stairs.

Exley abandoned the device in his hand for his pistol, this time remembering to click the safety off. Armise walked silently behind me, the only hint of his presence the ever-present feel of his eyes on me.

We climbed the stairs quickly. I didn't pause on the second floor, instead pushing through the soundproof door leading to the practice rooms. I breathed deeply, slowly, taking stock of my surroundings. Listening to the depth of silence above me. There was the shuffling of steps to my right as we stepped onto the third floor, and I swept my rifle in that direction. The hallway was empty, the door to the first practice room open, and I saw the side profile of a woman seated in a chair, her mouth gagged and her eyes wide. Her head snapped around as we approached. Tears streamed down her face.

But that wasn't what stopped me cold.

Armise slid around me and into the room, securing it and waving me inside. I willed myself to move, to keep the rifle hoisted to my shoulder even as my heart thundered in my ears.

Besides the woman secured to the practice room chair with those too-familiar metal cuffs over her wrists, the room was empty.

Armise stepped up to me, his body flush against my right and his back to the woman as he whispered in my ear. "Where is he?"

I cocked my head in the direction of the other room.

Ahriman was here. I had no doubt about it now. And we—I—had walked straight into one of his sick games.

"That's not your mom," Exley said in a low voice from behind me. "Fuck." He put his pistol back into the holster and ran to her, frantically working at the metal cuffs, trying to find a way to unlock them.

The woman struggled against the bindings, her wrists raw and seeping blood over the chair and into a pool on the floor. She bit at the gag, tried to force mumbled words around it. But I didn't need to hear her voice to know who she was.

I lowered my rifle. No amount of firepower was going to get us all out of this situation alive. "It's Sarai. The president's dead wife."

I heard Sarai's choked sobs, could see Exley becoming more out of control as he tried to locate the release. But my training kicked in and I went cold inside.

"Kersch knew," Armise nearly spat out.

I nodded. "Yeah, he knew."

It was the only conclusion I could come to. The president would have had her tracker taken offline when she died. And the identifying numbers could have been wiped from the database so that no one would be able to access her files. Her supposed death had come after an extortion attempt. There had been a very public funeral—a garish state affair that had put the president's stone-faced lack of grief on display—but no one had seen the body. Now I knew why.

The president had known that whether or not she was actually dead, he wasn't going to get her back alive. And he had publicly written her off so that no one could use her against him again.

As soon as Chen had brought the number of that unidentified tracker to him the president would have known. That the president hadn't made her recovery part of my mission, or even told me about her presence here, meant that he hadn't been planning for her to make it back to his bunker.

"Arrogant prick," I ground out. "Fuck that. We're getting her out of here too."

"Not quite yet." A voice came from behind me.

Armise and I spun, trained our rifles on Ahriman where he stood in the doorway.

"How long have you had her?"

Ahriman leaned against the jamb and crossed his arms. "Oh, it's been a while. Although she's in much better shape than your parents. You may want to get them to medical care soon."

I pulled the trigger on my rifle at nearly the same time as Armise did. But the bullets exploded against an invisible barrier and clattered to the floor.

Ahriman gave a feral grin. "New shielding technology. I'll have to let our scientists know it works."

Ahriman pushed away and disappeared around the corner, the sound of a metal door screeching open coming from the room next to us.

Armise sneered. "That is bad."

"I really fucking hate complications," I murmured. "Exley, stay with her. We'll be back."

Armise and I didn't have to discuss it. I took point as we crossed into the second practice room to find a man and a woman bound and gagged, standing next to Ahriman.

Both of their faces were beaten—purple and green of old wounds, the bright red of fresh blood. The woman's hair was matted, dirty and it appeared that the man's shoulder was dislocated. Their hands were bound in front of them at the wrists. Both of them were missing fingernails and they shook as if it was taking all of their effort to stand.

Ahriman gave both of them a shove in our direction and the woman stumbled and pitched forward. The man moved in front of her to keep her from falling to the floor. She was limping, and I could only assume from the odd angle of her knee that there was serious damage to that limb as well.

I didn't move.

Ahriman gestured to them as if he was presenting us a gift. "Go ahead, Armise. Take them. I won't stop you."

"And?" I asked.

Ahriman sat down in the PsychHAg torture chair and crossed his legs, tapping his fingertips on his knee. "I need a moment with you, Merq."

Next to me, Armise tensed.

The man—my father?—looked between Ahriman, Armise and me. His face was clinically blank. I knew from experience that it took years of practice to detach yourself thoroughly enough from a pain-racked body to appear that unaffected. It was a skill I had mastered in the training room next to this one. It had come more naturally to me than some of the other students. And surveying the man in front of me, I wondered if that was because I had a genetic predisposition for controlling my reactions and emotions.

I didn't recognize either of them by sight, though. There were features I could pick out—the color of the woman's eyes, the pronounced cheekbones and jaw of the man—that I could place with my own. But it wasn't enough. I had to be sure.

"Exley!" I called out.

I grabbed him by the arm when he walked in and placed him between Armise and me in a defensive position.

"That's them," Exley verified with shaky breath, his eyes flitting from my parents to Ahriman and back.

"Get them out of here," I instructed Armise.

My parents were silent as they moved together across the floor, feet shuffling, their progress awkward from the severity of their wounds. My father tipped his head in my direction, but his focus stayed on keeping my mother upright.

"I do not like this," Armise said in a whisper next to me.

"You think I do?" I replied, loud enough for Ahriman to hear. "Our mission was to return them to the president. Make sure that happens."

Armise gave me a clipped nod as Exley got my parents out of their bindings.

My father shook his head, wincing in pain as the gag fell from his mouth, and he stared me down but didn't say anything.

Almost thirty years since I'd last seen them and I knew I should've felt something, anything, for the people who had given me life. But I was most relieved to know that Armise would be walking out of here alive.

I tipped my chin up, signaling to Armise that it was time for them to go. Armise scowled deeply yet followed Exley and my parents out the door.

Ahriman and I waited for the sounds of their footsteps to fade away, then Ahriman stood.

"Come, Merq." He beckoned with his claw-like hands. "Let's talk."

Chapter Nine

"You recognize Sarai Kersch," Ahriman opined as we walked into the practice room where she was being held.

I didn't bother to answer him. I didn't want to know how long he'd been holding her or what had happened in the years she'd been missing. Those were details I didn't want to have in my head, available for the president to access at his will. Because if the president asked I would answer. I wanted to be able to tell him honestly that I didn't know.

Despite the president's apparent view that Sarai wasn't coming home, I was going to play this out with the intention of getting her out alive. I couldn't see any other option or consider that I wouldn't be able to.

Sarai was the president's wife, but she had never been involved in the dark deals her husband made for the Revolution. My contact with her had been limited to security detail or the handful of social occasions I was forced to attend for appearances as a Colonel for the Peacemakers. Regardless, I felt as if I knew her because of the president and how he spoke of her being his heart and his conscience. Of a love for her that couldn't be replaced. I'd never understood it. I had no frame of reference to believe that that type of unselfish love—love without an agenda—was possible. And it was in my power to give that back to the president. To return his wife to him.

I wanted to pretend that protecting her was simply a part of my job. She was a citizen and my job as a soldier was to protect those who didn't fight from the atrocities of war. I was willing to sacrifice just about anything or anyone—hell, even myself—for the president. But her life meant more than any ordinary citizen's because it meant something to him.

I studied the restraints. I didn't know where the release button was—if I had I wouldn't have been trapped in that chair for as many hours as I had in my year with the PsychHAgs.

One year of physical and psychological torture. Of seeing my blood spilled and flesh torn from my body as they wore me down. Sleep-deprived, starving, at the hands of men and women who fought on the same side that I did. My anger toward them feeding my drive to survive. I'd watched other members of my class being ceremoniously carried out in body bags, or slung across shoulders in disrespect for the ones who had broken way before they should have. We were forced to witness each death, each failure, and taught to learn from their mistakes. From their weakness. With each failure, the number of witnesses had dwindled until I was the only one standing in the practice room when my final classmate went into death with a howling wail that I could recall with perfect clarity.

I'd already been hardened, jaded many years before that, but my year here had nearly stolen the last of my will to live. I'd learned how to disconnect emotion from death. How to grasp at the last shreds of strength left inside me and endure mind-bending pain. To focus only on the mission and protecting the cause above all else. I wasn't a man. I wasn't a soldier, or even a number on their roster. I was a tool, and they were going to throw me into the fire and beat me into the fatal-edged sword they desired or allow me to shatter in the blinding heat.

They hadn't broken me, but they'd come close.

If the program hadn't been shut down that last day—the day I sat in this very chair, blaring music screeching in my ears, the whisper of PsychHAg Tiam feeding me lies and taunts while my blood flowed freely over those restraints—I would have been dead.

I had been saved by fate instead of my own strength. And that had been the greatest lesson they'd ever taught me.

Everyone had a breaking point—even me.

"Remembering your time here?" Ahriman gloated.

I snapped my head up and glared at him. He was using this room to set me off balance, and I was allowing him to do it.

"I survived."

And so will she, I thought, glancing at Sarai.

She was silent now, her wide brown eyes surrounded by the red of burst blood vessels, her hair matted with sweat, fingers gripping the chair with white knuckles. Her nails scratched over the metal as she flexed her hands, the restraints cutting deeper into her ravaged wrists.

I took a step toward Ahriman. I couldn't shoot him. Whatever shield he had would keep either a sonicbullet or a real one from taking him down. Which meant I was going to have to physically attack him. From years on the battlefield, I knew exactly how close I had to be to him to be within striking distance. I had no doubt that Ahriman expected it from me though. The only leverage I had was that he wanted me here for some reason.

I took another step, bringing me within nine feet of where he stood. His black eyes bored through me, unreadable as always.

"Where are we going with this?" I ventured, holding out my hands as if I was entreating an honest answer from him.

Ahriman tapped the gun at his side with those long fingers. I recognized it as a Colt—an ancient gun, not a replica. Where would he have gotten that?

"You've surprised me, Merq. And I'm not accustomed to being surprised."

I smirked. "How did I accomplish that?"

"By beating me at my own game. I may have allowed you to take that shot and assassinate the rather uncooperative premiere…" He paused and waited for a response from me that never came. I hadn't suspected that he knew about my real intentions, but now that he was verifying he had wanted me to kill the premiere I realized his move only made sense. Ahriman was the type of man who would never be satisfied with being second-in-command.

Ahriman turned and stepped closer to the chair. He ran a finger down Sarai's arm and she gasped, took in a long breath as her body shuddered from the touch. "Your exit from the stage was dramatic even for me. So many years in the planning, so easy to manipulate. And yet I couldn't see it all."

I kept my features and stance neutral as I worked his words over in my head. If I hadn't seen Armise's allegiance shift coming then Ahriman definitely wouldn't have.

"Armise."

Ahriman shook a bony finger in my direction. "Armise Darcan. The Mongol Giant. He won't come without you. I've learned enough to know that. I need him. But you? You're a side benefit."

"You had him here," I pointed out and took another step toward him. I was less than six feet away from him now.

Sarai's eyes swept between Ahriman and me, her hands balling into fists.

"I need him in Singapore. And someone convinced him to take that pesky transport chip out. So I'm doing a bit of rearranging. Your parents weren't enough leverage to garner your compliance. But Sarai—she's an innocent. I've seen the lengths you'll go to for Wensen Kersch. He is the one person you're loyal to above all else. That is a weakness. One I'm sure you're not proud of, but that exists nonetheless. Here's my offer. Her life for Armise. Simple."

"You'll kill him."

"He must be alive for what I need him for."

"Comforting," I snidely answered.

Ahriman chuckled at that. "Not in the least. You've served your purpose for them. They wanted a war and they have it. Now come to the winning side."

I crooked my eyebrow and took one more step.

"If I bring Armise to you, what could you possibly offer me?"

Ahriman made a *tsk tsk* noise, the sound of his tongue clacking echoing off the walls. "I really hate repeating myself. She lives and so do you."

"And Armise?"

"He lives." Ahriman put his hand on his pistol, gripped the carved handle and added, "For a time."

I dragged in the dry air, forced myself not to tense. Not to give away any physical tell of my intention to strike out at him. Sarai's eyes were glued to where Ahriman toyed with the gun.

"Last chance," Ahriman smirked.

Ahriman believed he was entitled. All-powerful and deserving of an unassailable right to decide who lived and who died. He didn't see any value in life besides his own.

I was only one step away from him now.

My anger churned within me, driving the accusation out of my mouth before I could stop it. "Why did you destroy the stadium?"

Ahriman smiled, all teeth and vengeance—a cold sneer that stopped me short.

"Because I could."

Ahriman had his gun in his hand before I could react. He popped off a shot, effortlessly placing the bullet between Sarai's eyes and propelling her head violently backward, taut against the restraints then sickeningly slack.

I froze. Watched her blood drip down the window behind the chair, heard the wet sound of shredded flesh dropping onto the floor.

"You are not in control," he roared, pointing the gun at me, inches away from my temple. "He is not in control."

I held my ground.

"Neither are you," I replied with steely calm.

Ahriman uncocked his pistol and put it back into his holster, that demonic exterior slipping away just as easily as it had taken him over. He shook his head. "Don't think you can trust him. There's much you don't know about the Mongol Giant."

My body nearly vibrated with the need to take him down. Saving Sarai was out of my control. I had failed her and the president. I would never let him have Armise. To accomplish that I would have to make it out of here alive. Or kill Ahriman first.

"And you do?" I retorted.

"It's my job to know, as it should have been yours."

"You're lying to me."

Ahriman chuckled again, the low unearthly sound jarring me. "Have you asked him about the key?"

I started. "Chen?"

Ahriman's lips tipped up, exposing his teeth in almost a snarl. "The other key."

I stepped up to him, putting us almost chest to chest. I ground my teeth together and balled my fists.

Ahriman didn't retreat.

"In case you're considering making an assassination attempt here and now, it would be good for you to know that I implanted a reverb in your father that will easily take out the president's bunker. I die and that bomb goes off. Counterstrike, I believe that's called. I assume that's where they were taken?" He tipped his head and studied me with inhumanly detached eyes.

"If you're going to allow me to just walk out of here, then we have nothing left to discuss."

Ahriman took a step back and swept his hand toward the door in a polite bow. "It's my only option now."

I turned on my heel without a word.

"Don't be complacent though," Ahriman said, stopping me. "I don't need technology to track you. No matter who dies, this is war. They're all disposable eventually. Inconsequential. And I won't be satisfied until I have it all. I'll go through them all to be the one left in control. And I mean one."

The fucker didn't know when to stop talking. His arrogance would be his eventual downfall. I would be his death.

I started for the door again.

"Merq," Ahriman called out as I turned the corner. "I wouldn't stray too far from home."

* * * *

I was seething as I descended the stairs.

I whipped out the in-ear radio device Simion had given me and switched it on. Static crackled over the earpiece and I pushed the button to open a communication channel.

"I need Neveed on the line."

"I'm here, Merq," Neveed's voice came out roughly from the other end.

"Ahriman put a reverb inside my father. Disarm it and make sure there's nothing else inside them. Either of them." I hesitated for only a fraction of a second, then, "And D3 this place. It doesn't need to exist anymore."

I didn't wait for a response. I ripped the device from my ear and stuffed it into my pocket.

By calling for a D3, I'd just given an order to detail, ditch and decimate this hellhole so it couldn't be used against us again. As far as I was concerned, everything having to do with the PsychHAgs had lost its credibility and effectiveness long ago. These former headquarters—these sun and pollution-bleached skeletons of buildings—weren't serving any purpose for the jacquerie or for us, so it was time for them to be ground into the dust.

Jegs was waiting for me at the foot of the stairs but I didn't stop to acknowledge her. Her presence on this mission wouldn't have made a difference, but I was loath to give her any forgiveness for disappearing to take care of her own business while the rest of us were putting our lives on the line for the cause.

I stormed out the front door of the PsychHAg facility and back into the dilapidated tent city. Jegs kept pace with me, remaining silent.

The Underground was still abandoned as we passed through it. The sun beat down relentlessly and the dust kicked up around us with a hot wind that made my skin itch.

I needed Armise. There were too many moving pieces for me to track them by myself anymore. We needed to talk. To have it all out and make sure there was nothing unsaid between us. Everything—even the concerns the doctor had shared with me—needed to be discussed so we could figure out our next move. I hadn't decided what I was going to share with Neveed and the president in my debrief. If they could hide information they believed I didn't need, then I had to consider doing the same.

Ahriman was after Armise. He'd been unafraid to let me in on that plan, so sure that I would willingly choose the president over Armise. That I had hesitated at all in making a decision between Sarai's life and Armise's had likely surprised him again.

I sighed.

Sarai. If it had been Simion or Jegs in that room Sarai would still be alive. Neveed would have done the same—giving Armise up without thought if he believed it would spare us any more bloodshed. But that was not an option.

"Why did he let you walk away?" Jegs said, her brusque tone betraying her belief that maybe it was me who had turned traitor this time.

I turned on her. "You get all your loose ends tied up?"

"Yes," she replied with a cold stare.

"Good. Then I assume your brother is either dead or he will be keeping the Nationalists in check."

"They're not going to engage us. And Grimshaw is meeting with the jacquerie leadership."

I stilled. If Jegs' brother Grimshaw was willing to meet with the jacquerie then there was hope that the Nationalists would swing to our side. It was an unlikely scenario, but more progress than Jegs had been able to convince her brother of before. "Maybe some good will come out of this clusterfuck of a day."

"He also gave me intel on the locations of some of the Committee members. As a show of good faith. Chen is working on it now."

"Right," I snorted and started walking again. "A show of good faith."

"Listen, Merq. You should know better than to question my loyalties by now—"

I gave a loud, derisive laugh that cut her off. "Should I?"

"We all have our connections that operate outside of the Revolution. Grimshaw is a Nationalist, but he is a populist at heart. He just believes that the power shift should come from order instead of chaos."

"Chaos is our order," I pointed out, not slowing my steps as we tramped through the dust of the camp.

Jegs grasped my biceps and yanked me back, stopping me. "But maybe it doesn't have to be. Look, he only wants peace."

I ripped my arm out of her hold. "And he believes the destruction of the infochip will bring peace?"

"He wasn't even alive then!" she protested. "The attack on those servers was done without spilling one drop of civilian blood. The Nationalists are seeking common ground, a righting of the fucked-up upending of our world. That was one tactic, put into motion over a century ago. They know we have the chip and they're not going to seek to take it from us or see to its destruction. Grimshaw has promised me that."

I took a deep breath, planted my feet and stared her down. "Is he talking to the Opposition just as readily as he is to you?"

Jegs froze, giving me my answer without her needing to say one word.

I stalked away from her and let loose a string of expletives that echoed through the empty camp. "He's working both sides, Jegs. You have to come to terms with that. And I have to know that if it comes down to him over us you won't hesitate."

"I could say the same of you," she replied with expertly restrained calm.

I balled my fists and ground my teeth together until I could feel pain radiating up my jaw and into my cheekbones. "Armise is with us now."

"Don't lie to yourself, Colonel. I've seen the way he looks at you. He is in this fight for you, not the cause."

"And I am in this fight for the Revolution."

Jegs shook her head and put her hands to her hips, looking away from me. Her fingers tensed and she pursed her lips before turning back toward me and saying, "I'm not so sure of that anymore."

Chapter Ten

"Where are they?" I said to Neveed as I barreled into the control room, my frustration having rocketed to anger on what should have been a short, uneventful walk back to the bunker.

Armise and Neveed were hunched over Chen, looking at something she pointed to on her screen.

Neveed's head snapped up. "The cells in the lower level."

I purposefully kept from looking at Armise, knowing that he could already read enough off me as it was. I wasn't ready to have it out with him. I needed to talk to my father before that happened, to see if he had any other information I could use.

"You're holding them?" I asked.

Neveed nodded. "Until we know more."

"Good."

I stalked out of the room without another word, even as Jegs pushed past me inside.

It didn't take me any time to locate the barracks this time around. I wound through the hallways, formulating my questions as I walked. Filtering the conversations around me at the same time, listening, taking information in, processing and analyzing it—my own internal monologue and the dozens of snippets of conversations I encountered. I did it without thought, without prompting or the need for orders. Maybe it was my training, maybe it was more. I'd never realized how many different threads I was able to follow in my head and still keep them all straight while simultaneously dissecting how they wound around one another.

I was in my element surrounded by noise—the chaos of battle, operations to gather intel, hostage negotiation and rescue, or D3 details.

It was in the spaces where I was left with too few stimuli that my mind began to cut out—the bombs, or Ahriman, for example. One track, one overwhelming stimulus. As if my mind operated like a parasite, snaking its tendrils in and grasping on to control. The more connections it maintained, the stronger it became.

I clomped down the steps to the lower level, passed the gym and headed for the cells in the back.

A soldier was stationed at each of the doors. They wouldn't be new recruits, but if they'd been given this detail they wouldn't be a high rank either.

"I need to see Lucien Grayson," I said without preamble, not giving a shit whether or not he knew who I was. "Which cell is he being held in?"

The guard narrowed his eyes and studied me then activated his comm chip. "General Niaz— Yes, sir." The guard swiveled on his heel and unlocked the door without another word, holding it open for me.

I crossed into the room and took the seat across the table from my father. He was dressed in a fresh Revolution uniform, his wounds stitched and bandaged and his hair wet and slicked back from his face. I hadn't had time to study him closely in the PsychHAg building. I took in as many details as I could without making it appear as if I was interested in anything more from him than answers.

He was just another man. I could find aspects of myself in his features—the cut of his cheekbones, the impassive glaze of his eyes, which were shaped the same as mine, but my eye color was all my mother. He was shorter than me by a couple of inches and not nearly as wide. His muscles were defined but not battle-hardened. The lines around his eyes and mouth were deep, as was the crease between his eyes. He had a prominent chin and a jawline that mirrored my own.

Besides that he was my father he was unremarkable. Maybe it was *because* he was my father that I found him unremarkable.

He tipped his head up in greeting and remained seated, leaning forward and steepling his fingers over his knees.

"Did you kill him?" he asked.

I slid out the chair across from him. I sat back, crossing my arms. "Aren't you more interested in whether or not Sarai made it out?"

Lucien shook his head. "He was never going to let her go. She'd been in Singapore for too long."

I frowned. "The reverb in your stomach was a minor issue to deal with first."

"Thigh," he clarified. "They implanted it into my thigh. Didn't even know it was there."

"Right," I said, indifferent.

He looked away from me and tapped his chin with his fingers. I could almost see him formulating his words in his head. "Armise," he finally said. "He isn't from the States."

"Singapore," I answered, not giving him anything else.

He didn't outwardly react, and I wasn't sure if that meant he'd already known the answer before asking it or if he had just as rigid a control over his reactions as I did.

"So this is going to be it between us? An information exchange?"

I choked out a laugh. "You're joking, right? I don't know you. I don't know her." I waved my hand in the direction of my mother's cell. "We share base DNA. And I'm not even sure how similar mine is to yours anymore."

Lucien leaned back, mirroring my position. It was a strategy used to pacify the person you were conversing with. An old body language technique that played up to our primal human instincts. That he was attempting to find a way into my good graces or to put me at ease had the opposite effect, setting me on edge instead.

"You're too young to remember a time when you could hunt anywhere around the capital," Lucien mused. "Shit, I'm too young. But your great-grandfather was a hunter. You resemble him greatly, in fact. He lived in one of the minor outlying islands to the south, off the coast, and learned how to hunt and fish from an early age. Even then the fish stocks were dwindling, so he would take his boat to the mainland and hunt with his father. Anyway, point is, my father liked to tell me stories about his father's experiences with apex predators. All the big game is gone now except in the Northern Territories and the Wildes of the UU, but at one time the apex predators were the animals that had no natural enemy—bears, lions, eagles. Those animals ruled their home territories. And, barring accident and injury, they were never hunted the way they themselves hunted. He was obsessed with the concept. About the hierarchy of the food chain, and our place in it. But his obsession was more than that as well. It wasn't animals he discussed the most. Because to him, the dominant predator, above all others, was humans."

"I see where this is going," I said with a sneer.

Lucien's eyes narrowed at my interruption. "I'm sure you do, but listen the fuck up anyway. Yeah, you get it. We're at the top of the survival chain. With no natural prey to take us out, except for one another. Dominant predator versus dominant predator. The point is, you and I share DNA but we also share more. That drive to live, to succeed. You're willing to go through anyone to achieve your goal, regardless of their status as another human being. And it's nearly impossible for you to fail. You're like that because I made you that way. Because your mother and I picked the best of our DNA and tweaked a couple other sets to make improvements. We created you. The ultimate soldier for our cause. Or so we thought. Apparently Singapore was doing the same thing. I don't know what the status of Armise Darcan is with the Revolution, but I can tell you definitively that he is dangerous. You keep him around and you will end up one on one with him. Dominant versus dominant…"

I held up my hand and faced my palm toward him. "Just fucking stop there. Please. Armise is the very least of your concerns, believe me. And how Armise and I end up positioned together should be even further down your list of worries." I scrubbed my hand over the scruff on my face. "Fucking hell."

He raised an eyebrow. "You're fucking him?"

"I can't see one way that is any of your concern," I growled. "You're sitting here telling me I'm genetmod, admitting to manipulating my DNA before birth—which is expressly outlawed—then you blather on about a relative I don't even know and who is of no importance to what is happening today and now, no matter how fucking fascinating his life was. You talk of me killing people with ease, without remorse, as if you know who I am, and you're worried about who I'm fucking?"

"It's a weakness that shouldn't be tolerated," he spat out.

"Then so is she!" I roared, pointing to the cell next door that held my mother.

"Don't give me that shit. He's from Singapore. Mainland, not one of the territories. Neveed told me who he is. You know Revolutionaries don't exist in that part of the world. How can you be sure he's not using you?"

I schooled my features and pulled myself back under control. "How can I be sure you're not?"

Lucien huffed, dragged his fingers over his lips and sat back. "Are you going to see your mother?"

I kicked the chair back as I stood, leaning my hands against the table so I was towering over him. "The president ordered me to bring you back. That mission is completed." And with that I stormed out of his cell, slamming the door shut behind me.

I walked back to the control room with only one thought in my head—to see Armise and get our conversation over with. There needed to be nothing hidden between us anymore. He was one of only two allies I could fully trust and yet he was the person my fellow Revolutionaries kept trying to drive me away from.

Either I was in too fucking deep with him to see the truth, or everyone else was too blinded by his birthplace to consider anything more. Both options were unacceptable. But this wasn't a distinction I could err on.

I wasn't going to allow anyone else to make that determination for me.

"Where do we stand with the Nationalists?" I overheard Neveed ask as I walked into the control room.

Jegs stood straighter, drew her shoulders back defiantly. "They're no longer a problem."

"I beg to differ," I interjected.

Neveed gave a clipped nod, acknowledging that he shared my opinion. "We'll continue to keep an eye on their movements."

"Armise told you Ahriman has shields that deflect real bullets."

Neveed dipped his head and tapped his foot nervously. "It's a complication."

I glanced at Armise. He was standing behind Neveed, his arms crossed. He gave a nearly imperceptible shake of his head.

"So what now?" I asked, steering the conversation away from the Nationalists.

Neveed picked up a piece of paper, which he started to hand over to me, but he stopped midway. I looked at the paper, then him, cataloging just how fatigued he appeared—his face was drawn, sunken, as if he hadn't eaten a proper meal in days or slept in that span of time. The circles beneath his eyes were dark even against his golden-brown skin. The worst were his eyes. Though they were normally strikingly focused and clear, he appeared to be having trouble finding anywhere for his gaze to land for longer than a couple of seconds.

"I have the coordinates of three of the Committee members. I need you and Armise to move on them now."

That had happened much faster than I'd expected. Maybe Jegs' brother was finally looking to create ties with the Revolution. If so, this was one serious peace offering. There were twelve Committee members for Armise and me to seek out and eliminate. Then there was Ahriman.

My anger took hold. That fierce determination that I was capable of stuffing down until it was needed. I thought about Ahriman killing hundreds of thousands of citizens in that stadium, of my fellow soldiers dying on States soil and in the DCR right now. Of Sarai.

I scowled and pulled the paper from his hands. The conversation with Armise would have to wait. It was time for us to go to work. I clapped Neveed on the shoulder, forcing him to look up at me and see that I wouldn't fail him in this. "We're ready."

Chapter Eleven

"Your second-in-command is losing it," Armise announced when we were on our way to our quarters alone.

"I caught on to that," I snidely replied, pushing past him into our quarters.

"Ahriman killed the president's wife," Armise said.

I had my back to him, but I knew he would catch the way my body stiffened at the mention of Sarai.

"Yeah," I answered softly, realization sliding through me that I hadn't attempted to filter the regret from my voice.

Armise came up behind, wrapped an arm around my chest and drew my back into him.

"How close are you to losing it?"

I bristled, that anger stirring in my gut, grounding me. Or maybe it was his arm around me, and the surety with which he held me. "I don't give a shit if he expected her to come back or not. I should have been able to get her out of there alive. I hesitated and she died."

Armise gripped me tighter. "He mourned for her long ago."

"Doesn't make it any easier," I confessed and pulled out of his grasp.

I began to shift through the closet, pulling clothes from the hangers and tossing them onto the bed. We would have to travel light, utilitarian, with small enough packs that we could be on the move constantly. We needed space for weapons more than clothes or any comforts of home. Those could all be procured for the right price. Weapons that we were comfortable operating—that were more like intimate lovers than one-night stands—were a necessity.

It didn't matter how unprepared we were at this exact moment—Armise and I had a job to do. One for which we weren't nearly as prepared as we would normally be. We would have to gather intel as we moved. To rely on sources and informants. Criminals and opportunists.

I discarded all of the clothes I'd thrown onto the bed, tossing all but what was needed into the bottom of the closet. We could make do with one other set of clothing—that was it. Everything else we would need to acquire as we moved.

The first two targets were in the continental United Union. In the same city, in fact. It was a stroke of luck that I didn't expect to last. It had taken only the amount of time for our walk between the control room and our quarters to decide that Armise and I would work separately but simultaneously, both of us completing our respective assassinations through means that would be considered natural or accidental. It was our best chance of keeping our agenda of wiping them all out secret. The Committee would already be on high alert. Waiting for attacks. But we would work decisively. Pick the known three off quickly and quietly. With some goddamn luck we could keep the remaining Committee members from going underground faster.

I stripped down to change into clothes that wouldn't be readily identified with any allegiance. Armise was at the table, laying his weapons out—the only knife I'd ever seen him carry, a pistol issued by the munitions officer and his sonicrifle.

"Are you picking up another rifle?" I asked him, pulling on a pair of pants.

He tracked my movements, openly surveying my body as I dressed. "Eventually. I haven't found one that fits right yet."

I nodded in understanding. You didn't choose the rifle as much as the rifle chose you. I had carried the same sonicrifle since becoming a Peacemaker. It had undergone modifications as technology improved, and repairs as it became as battle-worn as I was. Even now, with real guns being the preferred method of attack, I wouldn't give my rifle up. That didn't mean I'd be carrying it with me on this mission though. If Armise was going to bring his sonicrifle then I needed to be equipped with a real one.

That Ahriman was able to deflect real bullets as well as their sonic counterparts was going to make his death an interesting game. There were the usual methods of assassination outside of a gun—poisoning, knife to the spinal cord or heart, snapping the neck—all of which required being in close proximity to the target. Much closer than if Armise or I could get a clear shot from a distance. I didn't expect Ahriman to make it an easy task either way. As unsatisfying as it sounded, maybe our best option was to find out where he was and drop the largest reverb we could find directly over his head.

I didn't think I'd even mind being taken out from the blowback of that one if it guaranteed his death.

Armise and I were both prepared to die in order to eliminate Ahriman.

I expected to be gone months, if not the better part of a year, on this mission. Assassinating all twelve of the Committee members and Ahriman could take longer than that. Until then it would be Armise and me. Alone. Working together.

I stopped, frozen on the spot as that reality hit me.

I counted back the days. It had only been five days since I'd lain in bed with Armise the night before the Olympic opening ceremonies and lamented the idea that Armise and I would never be able to combine forces even though we would have made the perfect team. My life had changed more in the last five days than it had in almost twenty years—since I had first became a Peacemaker. I'd assassinated the leader of the Opposition, completed my long-standing mission and reignited the Borders War. I'd met my parents, watched the president's supposedly dead wife's head be blown open and explored the edges of my shifting relationship with Armise.

Armise.

Shit.

Out of every shock in the last five days, the discovery that Armise had gone traitor to Singapore and was my ally had been the most shocking. The most paradigm-shifting.

I rolled my shoulders, took in deep breaths, planted my feet and willed my body to relax. I repeated my mantra once under my breath then over again.

"I need—" I began to say, then realized I was answering a question Armise had put to me days ago. "Shit," I cut myself off, shaking my head.

Armise set down his knife, sliding it into the sheath, and placed it on the table. I stood at the end of the bed as he stalked toward me.

"Tell me what you need, Merq," he said evenly. Armise didn't appear fazed that it had taken me days to respond to him.

"Fuck. I need to touch you." I scratched my nails over my stubble, then over my hair, mussing it back. I'd thought before I'd spoken, but it didn't matter how I'd said it, I didn't want him to ask me why I wanted it. I was aware enough to know why it was him who I craved more than anything else.

There was too much I couldn't influence or manipulate. Too many secrets, too many people jockeying for power and for their own interests over the cause. I was bound by orders and a drive for retribution that threatened to consume me.

I needed to feel in control of one thing in my life. Just one piece, no matter how small. And nothing made me feel more powerful than controlling Armise Darcan's body. Having him at my mercy.

"I need…" I stepped up to him, putting us chest to chest. I kissed up his neck and along his jaw, then bit at his bottom lip. Armise gave a low moan. "To make you come."

Armise reached for my cock and I gripped his wrist, stopping him before he could touch me.

I rubbed my stubble against his freshly shaven cheek, dragging my lips against his skin, to his ear. "No. Only you."

Armise dropped his head to the side, giving me better access to his neck. "However you want it, Merq." He moved out of my grasp and flipped open the button on his uniform pants, slipping his hand under the material.

I pulled his hand away and dropped to my knees, pulling him roughly out of his pants and into my mouth without hesitation. He grew hard in my mouth, arching his hips toward me as he dropped back against the dresser, sagging into the furniture for support. Immediately he threaded his fingers into the strands of my hair, urging me forward until I was deep-throating his hardening cock. I slid my tongue up the vein as I sucked, fighting against the pull of his hands. I planted a hand on his hip, pushing him back and giving me room to swirl my tongue around the head and take him deep again.

Armise tried to force my movements and I tensed my muscles, fighting back against the insistence of his left hand in my hair and his right hand digging into my biceps. I worked slowly, stroking his shaft with deliberate teasing then rough abandon until he was impossibly hard, the skin stretching, balls drawing up tight in warning, even though I'd barely started.

I knew how to drive him to the edge fast and hard. But I also knew how to draw his pleasure out. How to make a blow job an excruciatingly ecstatic experience for him. And for me.

I took him in until the tip of his cock was pressing at the back of my throat and my lips were stretched around his base. Armise gave a wanton moan—a sound I rarely heard from him—and my desire kicked up, my need to see him unhinged thrumming through my body. I was just as hard as he was—maybe more. But I wouldn't come.

The competing instincts—being impossibly turned on while resisting the urge to take myself in hand and relieve some of the pressure—put every nerve in my body on edge. I needed to get Armise that keyed up. He released my biceps and fisted his right hand in my hair, closed both his hands, yanking my hair at the roots until the pain caused me to pull back and suck in a ragged breath.

I spared only a second to see his blown-out silver eyes—nearly black—close and his mouth open as he licked at his bottom lip. Then I sucked him in without warning and he bucked his hips up, trying to drive himself farther into my mouth. I dug my hands into his hips until my fingers hurt from the strain, until I could feel the press of his bones and wonder if I was holding so tightly to him that I would break the skin open. But Armise just kept pushing, fighting my hold.

I growled, the vibrations in my chest rumbling through me to where Armise's dick was buried deep in my throat. He wouldn't let up, wouldn't give in, and my frustration kicked up just as much as the desire, making me painfully hard. I took my hands off his hips, popped my lips off his cock, but before he could protest I lifted him off his feet onto the dresser and pushed him against the wall, my hand on his chest pinning him. I bent down and licked up his length with a long hot swipe then back down. Armise didn't have the leverage of his legs anymore and I grinned as I took one of his balls into my mouth and his head thwacked against the wall. I licked at them, mouthed them, ran my hand down his chest and to the base of his cock, gripping the length with a harsh pressure that had him letting out a litany of swear words.

From this position he was at my mercy. He put his palms on the dresser surface, sliding from the slick sheen of sweat over his entire body. He gasped for breath and his eyes were clamped shut, no longer able to focus on watching me work.

This.

This was what I needed.

I teased my tongue around the head of his cock, languidly, slipping the foreskin back to run my tongue along the underside then pulling just the head into my mouth and sucking so harshly that if I hadn't been holding him down he would have jumped off the dresser. I took him deep after that, fast, roughly. Hand, tongue and teeth grazing the silky flesh then nipping into it. His breathing came in labored gasps, my name a plea on his lips. His knuckles were white, gripped around the edges of the dresser as he desperately tried to pump his hips.

I scratched my nails down his torso, swallowed around him and he came apart, spilling hot down my throat as he groaned. I took it all in, my own cock pressing tightly against my pants, begging for release. But I didn't pull away. I floated in that space of his defeat, savoring the taste of his cum, the sight of his body sagging into the wall, all that strength leached from his body, ripped away by my lips, my hands.

Armise gave an audible exhalation of breath, then opened one eye and tipped his head in my direction. "Your turn?"

I gave one last swipe of my tongue across the head of his cock, which caused him to flinch and swat weakly at me. I stood up, wiping my lips with the back of my hand. I readjusted my aching dick, cracked my neck and gave him a smile. "Nah. I'm good."

Armise gave a low chuckle that washed over me just as surely as a caress of his hands. I bit at my lip ring, palmed my cock and seriously considered his offer. My dick hurt—there was no other way around it—but I used the pain to ground myself and focus. I put my amped-up energy into the task of gathering my weapons and making sure I had everything I needed organized into one small pack. Armise watched me silently for a while, then stood on shaky legs and shut himself into the en suite.

I heard the water running and splashing, then the creak of the faucet being shut off.

"I need to get a real rifle from the munitions depot if you're bringing your sonic," I noted, speaking louder so he could hear me.

The door to the en suite opened and Armise emerged—still half naked—wiping a towel across his face. Without his beard, and with his emotions this at the surface and unguarded, he looked years younger. I found myself studying him as if I didn't know him.

I knew his body, his movements. His strategy and method of attack. I could have picked out his voice among thousands.

And despite the unknown variables, I had no doubt in this moment that he was wrong when he'd said I didn't know him. There was nothing I didn't recognize. Nothing I couldn't see. There was nothing in our relationship for me to second-guess or mistrust.

I trusted Armise Darcan.

It wasn't as foundation-shaking an idea as I supposed it could have been.

Armise threw the towel back into the en suite then pulled on his pants. He walked to the table where his weapons were laid out.

"You could do that." He bent down and picked up a rifle case from the floor. He set it on the bed and flipped the latches. "Or you could take this one. I have a fondness for it. And I believe it is one you are proficient using." He smirked and handed the gun over to me.

I assessed the scarred barrel and stock well worn from use over centuries. I shouldered the rifle, looking through the scope, and gave a grunt of surprise when I realized why the rifle felt familiar. "This is the gun I used to assassinate the premiere."

Armise handed me a chest strap to attach to the rifle. "Happy birthday, Merq."

I took the strap and began attaching it to the barrel then the stock before I realized what he'd said to me. "I don't even know when my birthday is."

Armise chuckled at that. "It's today."

"I don't know what today is," I said honestly. "I don't pay much attention to days, or dates. Merely the passage of time, I guess."

"How do you know when you're supposed to be anywhere?"

"I just do." I shrugged. It was a question I didn't know how to answer because I'd never been able to understand others' reliance on physical reminders of time. I might not have known it was the anniversary of my birth, but that was because that date was of no consequence to me, therefore I didn't track it.

"You have never celebrated your birthday?" Armise questioned.

"You're fucking with me, right? And you have?"

"Every year," he said, his brows scrunched together. "There are Mongolian traditions I observe. Ones that I am sure are not as intended, but it is all I remember from my childhood. There aren't any records for me to know either way."

"Ah yes, the Mongol Giant," I said with just a hint of sarcasm.

Armise grumbled and crossed his arms. "Only one place you would have heard that name."

I frowned. "Ahriman had quite a bit to say about you. I'm inclined not to believe anything he said to me, or to at least filter it and decide what is real, what is manufactured, and what is manipulation."

"Let me save you some time. It is all manipulation."

"He said he needs you."

Armise leaned against the table his weapons were stacked on. "I am sure he thinks he does. I am more inclined to believe that I die the second I set foot on Singapore soil."

"He wants you alive. No, I think he said he *needs* you to be alive. At least for a time. He wants me to bring you to him, then I can fight for the Opposition."

At that Armise went silent for a heartbeat and I began to wonder if he knew why Ahriman needed him alive, but then Armise asked me something I didn't expect. "And what do you want?"

I lifted the rifle and slung it over my chest, adjusting the strap so it fit tightly enough to keep it fixed to my body but loose enough that I could turn it in my hands and easily bring it into the firing position. Satisfied with the fit, I turned to face Armise. There was only one answer. "To kill him."

Armise grinned. "You have any ideas about how to keep us plugged in without actually being connected to command?"

"Yeah. Chen used a design off the infochip. We'll have the Committee members' coordinates and intel loaded onto a chip that won't be connected to anything. We have to use a handheld reader to access the information and if we damage or lose the chip the information is gone. We're going to combine that with even more antiquated technology to map our progress, make sure we don't get lost traipsing through the continents. I'll ask her to create a series of star and topography maps for our most likely target locales. We'll be able to wear those maps on our forearms, underneath clothing. Of course those are not as readily updated as a communication chip. Communication with Neveed or the president is going to be non-existent. We'll rely on local informants and contacts to relay messages. But I suppose this is all normal procedure for the Dark Ops officer."

"You would think so." Armise shook his head, then waved his hand as if wiping the consideration away. "I adapt quickly. And anyway, I prefer to go into this op blind and off-grid. We do not need communication or transport chips."

"Good."

Maybe this partnering-up thing wasn't going to be as tough as I'd imagined.

Chapter Twelve

September 2258
Merq Grayson's 35th year
United Union – Amsterdam

I looked at the watch on my wrist then ran my hands over the stash of knives I had secured in various places on my body. I wouldn't need them if everything went according to plan. And there was no room for error in this kill or the one Armise was engaged in on the other side of the darkened United Union city of Amsterdam.

I couldn't believe two of the Committee members had remained in the same vicinity, let alone the same city, for this length of time. From the time that Grimshaw had handed over their names and locations to Jegs until Armise and I could get on the ground without the use of transport chips and without anyone tracking our movements, it had taken us nearly a month to cross from the East Coast of the States into the continental spread of the UU.

If all the intel we'd gathered hadn't pointed to them being two of the most inept members then I would have thought we were walking into a trap. Maybe their inclusion in the Committee had been a play by Ahriman all along as an early warning system. Tripwires of a sort. Because neither of them had moved or given any indication of being worried about their safety. We'd researched them for days, then surveyed them for another week, meeting with informants in darkened alleyways and abandoned storefronts. They were more excited about the prospect of these fools being bumped off than skittish about their complicit roles in the deaths.

Armise and I could have been complacent about the apparent ease with which these first two kills were coming together, but we were much better trained than that. Too experienced to fall for that rookie mistake. Armise and I knew what we were walking into.

These Committee member deaths—sure to be the easiest out of all the Committee members—were likely designed to set the surviving members on alert. I didn't expect any sabotage, any attempt to save the man and woman. They were being led to the slaughter so that the others could escape the executioner's blade while we were occupied.

Which meant that Armise and I had to make these first two deaths appear as innocuous and accidental as possible, so that none of the remaining members would know we were on our way for them as well.

For my old and infirm female target, I was using poison that would cause an instantaneous heart attack. For Armise's mark, a murder-suicide supposedly at the hands of the man's mistress. They were old tricks. An assassin's grab bag thousands of years old, passed down through stories told by brash military recons attempting to one-up one another. By the whispers of legends that were infinitely more interesting than tactical battle manuals. Or by inebriated witnesses and spotlight-seeking gossips in dank bars. I usually found the latter were the most reliable.

Regardless of the source, these tactics had continued on because they worked. It would be our job to never be spotted, to leave no question as to the complete lack of originality and intentionality of their passing, despite their similar timing.

We were hoping that the nearly simultaneous natures of the kills would help sway opinion as well. Assassins rarely worked in pairs. Ahriman knew we were working together, but he was unlikely to raise any noise that could point us in his direction. I was sure that no matter how many Committee members we picked off, Ahriman would remain silent and unexposed.

While the president craved being on the front lines, Ahriman would be concealed behind them in layer upon layer. Ranks of soldiers, officials and decoys masking his true location.

He would be the most difficult target to get to, but we had twelve others to eliminate before him. And I wasn't going to do anything that would jeopardize my ability to get to him in the end.

The light flipped on in the house in front of me and my target descended the stairs leading into the kitchen. She looked worn down, haggard, and I was sure it wasn't just the late hour that gave that impression. When I'd seen her just over a month ago at the opening ceremony, she'd been in an elegant gown of black with threads of shimmering purple, reflecting the colors of the UU, her home country. Her age and failing health had been obvious then but allayed by a light in her eyes and a triumphant smile—both of which were decidedly absent now.

She shuffled through the kitchen, her body hunching into itself. She was alone, as she had been since her partner had learned of her decision to actively work for the Opposition. She had made her decision and it had cost her her family and her health. Soon it would also claim her life. But this ending was going to be more mercy than vengeance.

She turned on the faucet, holding a glass under the water, waiting for the liquid to cool. I slipped the injection device out of my pocket and pumped the mixture into where I'd tapped into the shared purified water line for the string of grandiose houses in the neighborhood. She slipped the glass under the flow, filling the cup and taking the liquid back greedily. Her heart treatments made her inordinately thirsty. She wouldn't have to worry about the treatments or the overwhelming thirst for long.

With a half-life of ten seconds, the heart-attack-inducing poison was engineered to break down in water—even the water molecules within the bloodstream—and be completely untraceable in less than a minute. The nanoparticles within it had been modified to bind only to her DNA, so it didn't matter that the toxic mixture was spreading to all the houses in the area. She would be the only casualty of the poison tonight.

I coolly witnessed the moment her heart seized in her chest—her hands clutched at the fabric of her nightgown and her eyes went wide with surprise and pain. The glass clattered back into the sink and she dropped to the floor with an audible wheeze.

I took the handheld medical sensor from my pocket and switched it on, remotely monitoring her vitals. She was in cardiac arrest, but with the dosage of poison I had given her she should have died almost immediately and somehow she was still hanging on. I swore under my breath. I watched the erratic heartbeat continue to stutter but stubbornly refuse to quit on the monitor screen. Well, didn't that just fuck over my plan. Now I was going to have to enter the house and make sure she didn't make it anywhere to call for help.

I closed the access plate to the water system and snuck around back to the exterior door. Her security system was useless, lending credence to her low place on the Committee's roster. I used the maglock key duplicated from her cleaning company and entered to only the creaking of the house settling around me.

I pulled a knife from a holster at my thigh and waited to see if there were any other noises coming from elsewhere inside. We'd been guaranteed that there would be no one else present. As if I would trust any of that intel or bet my safety on it. I heard a gurgling noise coming from the kitchen. The poison had taken her to the ground immediately but the heart attack hadn't quite finished her off yet.

The kitchen was lit with only one low light that hung directly above where she lay, spotlighting her desperate pulls for breath and the feeble kick of her feet that was more death throes than protest. Her attention didn't turn to me when I entered the room—I guessed she probably didn't even know I was there. I crossed the tiled floor and knelt at her side, listening to her slowing respiration. Her pupils were dilated despite the bright light shining in her eyes and her lips opened and closed but no sound came out.

I sat on the floor and waited for her to die.

I knew her name even if I didn't want to speak it or think it. I knew every aspect of her life—even the details she had probably hoped no one would ever know. I was the sole witness to her passing. I kept a vigil of the damned. One soulless being ushering another past the gates of hell.

Her eyes didn't close, and she made no further sound. She simply stopped breathing. And still I waited. I had to be sure before I left the body to be discovered at a later time.

I pulled the radio out of my pocket and switched on the device, leaving the channel open for Armise's confirmation on his kill.

Five minutes later the code came through. Two clicks on the receiver and one extended tone. I repeated the pattern back and shut the radio off.

Two down.

Ten to go.

Then Ahriman.

* * * *

I heard the president's voice in my head urging me to stay focused on the task at hand. To not rush our work. So I took the time to make sure my presence here wouldn't be detected. I lingered longer than I would have advised any trainee, but I trusted my instincts, and getting this first kill right was worth the risk.

I flipped my hood over my head as I exited the house and crossed the property, cutting across the neighborhood. Armise and I were set to meet up at a Revolution safe house downtown. He'd taken a cycle to travel to his target, but I'd decided to go on foot. I wanted to see the city, to witness exactly what was happening on the ground.

Armise had been right when he'd asked snidely where I'd been to not know what the average citizen's life was like. I'd been unable to shake the idea that not knowing was another failure on my part. No, it was a glaring oversight.

I'd allowed myself to be coaxed up the mountainous belief system of the Revolution without looking around first to see if there was a different way—perhaps an easier way?—to get to the same spot. Then I'd willingly jumped, falling, careening into the narrative built by the Revolution. And while their version of events was more accurate than what the Opposition attempted to portray, I should have been smart enough to see that no one source could provide all the intel I needed.

Shit, wasn't that the point of the infochip in the first place?

The Opposition relied on the belief that in the absence of knowledge, in that void created by ignorance, there was room for dishonesty. Ahriman knew that if he controlled education and access to dissenting viewpoints, then there was less likelihood of an insurgency rising against him. And we as a society were willfully following that path. We were allowing our history to be rewritten and presented in pieces that strengthened one point of view because we had no reason to think otherwise.

The Revolution was guilty of the same desecration. What limited knowledge I'd been able to glean growing up had come from sources definitively tied to the Revolution. But it was the president who had first influenced me to look beyond what I was told.

'Just because you haven't seen it for yourself, felt it or experienced it, doesn't mean it doesn't exist,' he used to say to me.

Then Armise had come along and dragged me back to the top of that metaphorical mountain and forced me to look around.

Fuck. Why had it taken me this long to figure that out?

For too long I'd been blind, closing my eyes and ignoring all dissension that didn't have to do with my mission. I'd shut myself off, been bound by a narrative that affirmed what I was told instead of examining it for myself. And I couldn't deny that Armise had been the one to free me from that ignorance.

I stuffed my hands in my pockets and moved into the city proper, staying in the shadows cast by the flickering street lights. Amsterdam was a city recently rebuilt. It had been completely destroyed by floods over two hundred years ago. What was left of the old parts had been swallowed by the sea when the dykes were attacked in the twenty-fourth century. From what little I'd heard, I knew that the current layout mapped almost exactly to the previous incarnation. The buildings were constructed of stone dug out of the ground in pits from the mountains of the UU instead of the wood that had been the primary building material at one time. The rough-hewn stone gave the city an aura of timelessness. Of not belonging to this era. I could easily pick out the modern architectural touches—the gravity-defying slant of polymaterials, the shine of manufactured metals—but those were merely touches in the overall aesthetic.

Tent cities didn't exist here the way they did in the States' capital. The poorest citizens had moved out of the city after the floods and created self-sufficient encampments in the country, well above sea level.

Tonight the streets were crowded despite the late hour, since active combat had yet to hit this part of the world. But it wouldn't be long before these citizens were barraged with the firefights and bombings that came with our power struggle. I felt the nervous anticipation in the people who rushed through the streets.

I'd heard that Amsterdam was a city of revelers. I'd seen the footage of celebrations the night of the opening ceremonies. But the mood of the citizenry now was decidedly restrained and on edge. There were also visual cues to the imminence of the war. The sunburst symbol of the Revolution was graffitied on the ground and on stone walls, the ink still dripping from the most recent tags.

The downtown wasn't a place where people lived, from what I'd quickly learned in our surveillance of the Committee members. The heart of the city encouraged commerce, hosted travelers and served as a crossroads for those on the move. The shops reflected that purpose, hocking food to go, supplies and treated water. In the section I was walking through there were dozens of comm cafes and adverts for guides, which was thinly veiled code for the men and women who could get you anything you needed or desired—black market or legal—for a steep price.

I turned down an alley next to a bar and considered stopping for a drink, but the most dangerous substance I'd ever put in my body was surge. And as addictive as it had the potential to be, every time I ingested it was under the watch of a Revolution doctor.

I didn't do the escapism thing. Couldn't buy into a mindset that sought out a way to dull the senses.

Shit, and maybe—I realized with sickening certainty—that was because I was shutting myself off to all the emotions normal citizens felt.

What the fuck was I doing to myself?

It was infinitely easier not to think. Not to feel. Not to question the narrative that propelled my existence to an unseen—but likely bloody and martyred—ending.

I was a soldier. That should have been enough. But since Armise had appeared in my life, I'd been steadily slipping away from that as my primary identity.

I came around a corner into a brightly lit section of town, the buildings swished in vibrant paint trails of reds and oranges, and loud bass-heavy music pumping out of speakers attached to the street light poles. The streets were just as packed here, but with an air of joviality that had been missing elsewhere. Next to me a hand-drawn sign advertised piercings, tattoos and body mods.

I'd gotten my first piercing—the one in my lip—as part of an undercover op when I was eighteen. Since then I'd added the barbell in my eyebrow and the line of hoops in my left ear. I couldn't deny that I liked that first shot of pain when the needle pressed through my flesh. I enjoyed the sensation of the cool metal against my skin and the weight of the piercings, as minuscule as they might be.

I was alone. On a different continent from my superiors. Untrackable, unattached. Unfettered, even if not free. And I had the overwhelming desire to mark the moment. Maybe it was time for another piercing.

The door to the shop was propped open. Warmed, purified air pumped out of the storefront in billows as it hit the chilled night. I walked through the cloud and was greeted by a man at the front desk, his head shaved and a pattern of black and gold anchors on his forehead.

"*Ha'jour,*" he greeted me.

While Continental English was spoken by almost everyone here as a second language, I decided to switch to the seaboard dialect of this part of the UU. "*Je'il voudrais en piercing tekrij.*" I'd like to get a piercing.

He tipped his head in the direction of a woman with long blonde hair and a thin frame. "Ezme can help you." A line of delicate, curved silver barbells ran up her arms, down the line of her collarbone, and dipped into a V-shape that followed the edge of her low-cut shirt.

I sat down in the chair next to her and removed my hood. If either of them knew who I was they didn't show it. Of course, Amsterdam was known for living on the fringes of modern society, for discretion and favoring cash above all else. I was sure to be recognized, but it was unlikely that anything would come of it.

"What are you thinking?" she asked, pulling on a pair of sanitized gloves.

I quirked my eyebrow. I hadn't thought that part through, so I went with my first notion. "Nipple."

"Both?"

"No, just the left."

"You can put your jacket and shirt over there." She motioned to a table next to the chair.

I stripped off the jacket and pulled my tee over my head then settled back.

"No tattoos," she remarked, gliding a cloth used for sterilization over my chest.

"No."

"You ever think of getting marked?" the man leaning on the desk asked.

"Yeah. Just haven't gotten around to it."

"It is a quiet night," the man stated, gesturing outside with a smirk as the raucous music blared into the night air. I couldn't restrain a smile. "My chair is open for hours. Much damage can be done in that amount of time."

I laughed. "True."

"What is your vision?" he inquired.

"I don't have one."

He gestured to the scar on my shoulder that had come from the repairs done after the DCR standoff. "You are already marked in very permanent ways. Perhaps there is a story there."

More than I cared to share. I tried to formulate an appropriate response that would convey what I was trying to say in his language. "*Je veronderstel que j'heb geleefd par de balkoo.*" I suppose I've always lived by the bullet.

He nodded thoughtfully and lifted a BC5 screen from the desk. "Let me draw something for you."

Ezme pulled open a drawer, the thick medicinal scent of medical-grade antiseptic filling my nose.

"What gauge?"

She started to hand a tray of hoops and barbells to me, but I waved it away.

"The same shape as what's in my lip, a couple gauges larger. Just make sure it's not titanalloy."

She plucked a hoop off the tray and showed it to me. I nodded and she wasted no time placing the metal clamp around my nipple then swiping the needle through immediately after. That familiar sizzle of heat and pain rushed through me, morphing into a slow dull burn, followed by the rush of endorphins that turned the uncomfortable sensation into one of arousal. The removal of the needle and her practiced movements inserting the hoop only intensified the effect and I had to suck in a deep breath of the warm shop air to bring myself back down.

"Beautiful," she said to me with a shy smile. She fastened the ends together and secured the piercing.

I closed my eyes and sat back while listening to her clean up. My chest throbbed, ached, and now that the hoop was in all I could think about was what the coolness of Armise's chest would feel like against mine.

Speaking of Armise, he was probably wondering where the fuck I was.

Or maybe he wasn't. What did I know?

Even though we'd spent almost two months now in close quarters, not much had changed between us. We planned, researched, strategized then ate, fucked and slept. We orbited around each other, came together then bounced away again, testing, watching, assessing.

Armise didn't push me like he had in the president's bunker. He barely spoke to me outside of our tactical conversations. Maybe he'd finally tired of me answering his questions with more questions.

He disappeared for hours at a time and I rarely woke up with him next to me. But all of this was more normal than not.

"Take a look," I heard the man call out. I opened my eyes and got up from the chair.

The man flicked his wrist and turned the BC5 screen in my direction. On it flickered a black and white image of a bullet with a thick rope coiled around it.

"Perhaps it could go over your shoulder," he offered, popping the screen up and manipulating it to arch over my scar and show me what the tattoo would look like.

I shook my head. While the design was perfect in a way that I could feel more than explain out loud, the positioning of it needed to be elsewhere. I turned my back to him. "Not over my shoulder. Ink it over this scar."

The man gave a low whistle as he took in the jagged and dimpled slash that ran from my left shoulder diagonally almost to my spine.

I studied the drawing again. "And add a knife to it."

"I can do that. Let me shift the image a bit." He flicked the screen down to the desk level, his brow furrowing in concentration.

I watched him work, his fingers dancing over the semitransparent screen. As he enlarged the bullet, making it slightly thinner and longer, it hit me why the design had immediately felt right to me.

"Why did you use a .22 caliber rifle bullet?"

The man cracked his neck then wiped the screen off his desk, dismissing it. He hitched up his sleeve, revealing the reddened skin of fresh ink and the image of the Revolution's sunburst. He ran his finger over the tattoo then looked to Ezme. She nodded her agreement to whatever he was silently asking, and apparently that was enough for him.

He pulled his sleeve back down, then said, "Let me show you something." He walked around me and beckoned for me to follow him into the back room.

We passed under the air filter pumping out that warm, humid air and the temperature dropped as soon as we crossed the threshold.

"I thought I recognized you when you walked in, but the scar on your shoulder was when I knew," the man said with a smile. "That is the one you got in the DCR during the war, yes? I saw a profile of you for the Olympics and… It does not matter. There is another element I think we could add to your mark."

We entered a cramped office and the man shut the door behind us, bolting it closed. I tensed and he retreated with his hands up. "No harm meant. I must be careful with what I'm going to show you."

I unclenched fists I hadn't realized I was balling up, my self-protection instinct taking over without thought. I nodded. "Okay."

He moved to the bottom corner of a line of shelves, crouching down and reaching his hand into the clutter. Then an audible pop came from behind me. I turned to find a section of the wall cracked open.

The man walked around me, pushed the door open and grasped an unseen item with two hands. He unfolded the dark, dusty cloth from around it and held it out for me to see as he flipped it open.

I stared, disbelieving. I wanted to ask him where he had gotten it. How long he had had it.

The book was in an advanced state of deterioration, the pages cracking and crumbling at the edges. Its cover was made of a soft, brown material worn down at the spine and the place where fingers were most likely to touch. Where hands had been touching it for what had to be hundreds of years.

It was the first real book I'd ever seen.

This man, in a tattoo parlor in a seedy part of Amsterdam, had no idea what immeasurable peace he had just handed to me. I'd always been sure that not all the paper records had been destroyed, but until now I'd never seen proof of their actual existence. I had no doubt that the man understood the danger of protecting this book. Any and all paper records discovered were to be delivered to the authorities for 'safekeeping,' and it was illegal for any citizen to have them in their possession.

If this book existed, that meant others did as well.

"You said you live by the bullet, but it is more than that. You are bound to us, to the citizens you protect. You offer your life for us. That is why I added the rope. Tell me, where does the scar come from that you want to cover?"

I couldn't take my eyes off the book, and I answered him more honestly than I would have otherwise. "From an incident much like the DCR. This one had a much different outcome, however."

He nodded gravely, appearing as if there was something else he wanted to ask but couldn't.

"What is it?" I prompted him.

"A knife, a bullet and a rope—all items that can be used to kill. To take life. And yet they are our only weapons against tyranny and for freedom."

I crossed my arms and took a step back. "They're not our only weapons," I said with surety. "May I?" I asked, tipping my head toward the book.

The man offered it to me with arms outstretched. I gingerly took it from him, afraid to touch the pages as he had or risk damaging them further. He stepped up next to me and delicately flipped the pages. It appeared to be a handwritten record with scrawled passages and etched line drawings. I could see the indentations where the person had put pen to paper.

"It is the journal from a soldier from the First World War, at the beginning of the twentieth century. There is a particular drawing, an entry about a man he met in the midst of fighting. Here." He stopped on a page and pointed to a section. "My Continental English is not practiced, but Ezme knows enough that she has been able to read it for me. He talks about meeting a fellow soldier, and although they were of different worlds, and had been brought together by violence, they formed a friendship. This drawing here is of a language neither Ezme nor I can decipher. But the text below indicates that it means 'bound'. You and I, and all Revolutionaries, we are not the same, but we are bound by something greater than our differences."

"I want that added to my mark," was all I could find the voice to respond.

"I suspected you might," the man said with a grin. "Do you want to look at it more?"

I shook my head. At that moment I didn't trust the stability of my hands with such a delicate resource.

The man didn't appear to be put off by my refusal. He just took the book from my hands and shut it carefully, wrapping it with care then placing it into the space in the wall. When he clicked the door shut there was no visual evidence of the hiding place.

"Then let's get started," he said and led me back to the front room. "You want to take a hit before I start?" he asked as I straddled the tattoo chair.

"Of surge?"

"Not exactly," he clarified, snapping sterilized gloves over his hands. "The black market stuff. Working over this scar is going to be painful." The tattoo artist ran his fingers over the raised ridge along my back. "On second thought, if you survived whatever did that, I do not think it will be needed."

I grinned. *Whoever stitched it,* I wanted to correct him. This guy had no idea the amount of pain I could tolerate. The hum of the tattoo needle buzzed in the warm air and I thought I was ready for the sting, but the first prick of the tattoo needle to the scar nearly sent me out of the chair.

The man stopped. "Surge?"

I breathed heavily. "No. The pain is good."

"Okay."

I closed my eyes, wrapping my arms around the headrest and putting my chin on my forearms. I sank into the pain, allowing it to wash through every nerve, and forced my breathing to slow so that my muscles would relax.

"This was not part of the plan," a voice came from behind me, snapping me out of my headspace.

"How the fuck did you find me?" I gritted out to Armise, not turning my head.

The tattoo artist's needle went silent. I flexed my shoulders, the soreness of the abused skin traveling down my back in dull waves.

"I do not need a fucking chip to track you."

I nearly laughed at the frustration in his voice. It wouldn't have been easy to locate me in a city of this size, but leave it to Armise to find a way.

"We okay here?" Ezme asked in Continental English.

I nodded and settled back into position. "Go ahead," I prompted the tattoo artist.

That metallic hum started up again and the needle dug into the scar, sending fresh spears of pain down my spine.

There was the scraping of chair legs on the floor and Armise appeared in front of me, sitting down facing me, his elbows on his knees, leaning forward.

I looked up at him, scanned his face and body for any hint of injury from the kill he'd just completed, but he was unmarked. I didn't bother introducing him to Ezme or the tattoo artist. If they knew who I was then it was likely they knew who Armise was as well, even if he no longer wore the distinctive black and silver beard that had been a hallmark of his persona during the Olympics. If either of them were affected by his appearance then they didn't show it. Ezme sat in the piercing chair, twirling her blonde hair between her fingers as she flicked through images on a BC5 screen. And the tattoo artist's hands seemed as steady as they had before as he etched the image into my skin and swiped away the excess ink.

"We good?" I asked Armise, switching over to a dialect of northern Singaporean I assumed neither Ezme nor the man would understand.

Armise raised an eyebrow, studying me. It was the first time I'd spoken anything besides Continental English with him, and I was speaking Mongol. His home dialect.

"We're good," was all he responded, in the same language.

I sucked in a breath and ground my teeth together as the artist worked over a particularly sensitive spot. I kept my eyes locked to Armise and watched as he appeared to mimic the movement, as if he were feeling the same pain. Then I remembered the lightning bolt on his back—the tattoo that covered a wound I had given him—and realized he probably knew exactly what I was experiencing.

"We need to move after this," I said, still speaking in Mongol.

Armise ran his fingers through his hair, smoothing an errant strand back. "They recognize us."

I nodded. "They're okay, but the next ones may not be."

Armise got up from his chair and walked behind me, watching the tattooist work.

"Anything else I should know about?" Armise mused.

Solely from the clipped tenor and annoyance in his voice I could picture the way he was standing—legs wide, arms crossed, likely a scowl tipping his lips down. The tattoo artist pulled away for a moment and I ventured a glance over my shoulder to find Armise in that exact position.

I grinned. "I got my nipple pierced too."

The muscle in Armise's jaw ticked and he shifted from one foot to the other. He inhaled sharply, uncrossed his arms and ran both his hands through his hair. He gave a mumbled "fuck," and ran his tongue over his bottom lip.

I chuckled and settled my chin on my arms again, satisfied with his reaction. It was good to know that I could still surprise Armise as much as he could surprise me.

Chapter Thirteen

The man's blood splattered across my face, dripped warm down my cheeks, and I had to retreat a step to keep his blade from slicing through my abdomen. I flipped my blade from my right to my left hand and drew the length across his arm. He screamed, backed up another step, then came at me again.

Where the fuck was Armise?

I shouldn't have needed to be in this house in the first place. Shouldn't have ended up in hand-to-hand combat with our target. But his bodyguards had stubbornly refused to let me into the safe room the Committee member was keeping himself locked in. So I'd had to take them all out first to even get to the wily asshole. I'd opened the door with the cooling fingerprints of one of the dead bodyguards then promptly been jumped by the Committee member.

Everything our intel had told us pointed to him being a spineless idiot, much like our first two kills. We'd known the bodyguards were there and the house was on lockdown, but the plan had been simple. Well, it would have been if we'd known that this particular

Committee member was so paranoid that he hadn't left his safe room in days. I supposed he had had good reason for that paranoia though.

I'd at least been able to drive him into the living room with floor-to-ceiling windows overlooking the bay. With Armise set up with his sniper rifle in the hills, I'd given him plenty of time to pop off a clean shot. But as the seconds then minutes dragged on and I steadfastly took weapon after weapon off this guy and he kept coming at me, I wondered if that shot was ever going to come.

The guy had to be hopped up on surge or some other drug because he was stronger than he should have been. Faster than he should have been.

Should have. Fuck. Those words were going to get me killed by an Opposition pissant.

His eyes were beady and dangerously focused for how untrained all our intel had led us to believe he was. But I could see him tiring as he circled me again, his shaking arm dripping blood onto the black-tiled floor. His movements were erratic, the desperation evident in the droop of his shoulders and the heaving of his chest.

If I'd had a comm chip I would have told Armise that now was the time to take his shot. But I didn't have the fucking chip and my hands were otherwise engaged, keeping my radio—my only communication method with Armise—out of reach in my pocket.

So I kept him moving, waiting for either the whizz of a sonicbullet or the pop and shattering glass of a real one.

There was some reason that Armise wasn't taking his shot and I was either going to have to gut this guy and finish him off or risk taking on an injury that could leave me vulnerable. The only thing I could fathom was that no matter where I moved in the room Armise couldn't sight the target.

"Even if you kill me you won't win," the man gurgled, the place where I'd swiped him across the neck sending another spray of blood down his chest.

Now he was just annoying me.

"Fuck this," I grumbled. I dropped onto my haunches, hopefully clearing myself completely out of Armise's sight line.

It only took a second, then the glass behind me was raining down around me, sprinkling to the lacquered floor, and the Committee member dropped with a definitive thud.

I stood and glared out the window at where the bullet had come from. If Armise still had his eye to the scope then he would see the annoyance painted on my face.

I checked the man's vitals to ensure he was dead—although with the gaping wound that started at his cheek and blew out the back of his head, I was relatively sure he wasn't coming back.

I swiped my blade clean on the Committee member's uniform and placed it back into my sheath, then stormed out of the house. My fury grew as I tromped up the hill. I hated fucking complications and this op had been nothing but since the beginning. I was ready to take it out on Armise, but that asshole was the one to start yelling first.

"What the fuck was that?" Armise growled at me as he stepped out from behind the cover of a water purification shed, slinging my rifle over his shoulder.

"Me?" I yelled back. "It took you fucking long enough to take the shot."

"Maybe because someone's head kept getting in the way. Forgive me if I didn't want to fucking explode your brain as well!"

"I gave you plenty of opportunity to shoot! He fucking came at me with a knife. That tiny-ass surge-freak came at me with a knife!"

Armise barreled down on me and gripped my chin in a vicious hold, craning my neck back. He let go just as quickly, snapping my head down as I jerked away from him.

Armise gave a wicked grin. "I don't see any fucking marks on you."

I huffed, my anger ebbing despite wanting to hold on to it. "Because I'm a goddamn professional," I snapped.

Armise's shoulders shook with silent laughter. He pulled a cloth from his medkit and threw it at me. "Clean yourself up, soldier."

I wiped the cloth across my face and down my neck, the blood already beginning to dry into a sticky mess.

"Water?" I asked, looking up at Armise where he paced in front of me.

He handed a canister over to me and I cracked the top, wetting the cloth.

"So what the fuck did happen?" I pushed him.

"I told you. I could not get a clean shot."

I arched an eyebrow. "Couldn't without putting me at risk, you mean?"

"I would think that would be of some import to you," he replied flippantly.

"Fuck that. You could have compromised the mission. You're the one who said this war goes on whether we live or die."

Armise's nostrils flared and he cracked his neck. "I am also the one who said my loyalty is to you, not to any of them. We stand together on this. There is no other option. Not for me."

I glared at him, silent. Tried to grasp hold of the emotions his words almost ripped free from me. I could feel a response inside me. As if my reply should be automatic and just as determined as his was. There was something unnamed there, something I had never experienced and didn't know how to describe, but before I could grasp hold of it, it was gone. "I don't want to have this conversation."

Armise fisted his hand in my shirt, yanking me forward. "You think I do? Talking to you is fucking pointless. But this"—Armise palmed my cock, the heel of his hand digging into the base of my dick while his long fingers began to work me over—"this at least you can understand. This you know how to respond to. With this, at least I can get an honest fucking reply."

I ground my hips into his hand. "Is this the kind of response you want?"

Armise didn't answer me with words. He slipped his hand beneath my waistband and gripped my cock, slowly pumping it.

The adrenaline from the kill was still flowing through me, thrumming through my blood, and yes…this was a reply I could give him. I threw my arm over his shoulder and buried my lips in the curve of his neck, biting down on his collarbone then licking up the tendon at the side to his ear.

I fit my body against his, pushed him back on his heels with the force of the movement. He rocked into me, snaking his hand behind my neck and threading his fingers through my hair.

"We should probably take this elsewhere," I whispered against his skin.

Armise responded by tightening his grip on me. "Fuck it. They're all dead."

I pushed him against the shed, rutted up against him, kissed at his neck, along his jaw then found his lips. Fuck, those lips. Soft and yet demanding. That thick bottom lip, begging to be bitten at, my piercing catching on his skin until he opened for me. And that first slide of his tongue on mine was better than any drug, more satisfying than any kill.

He popped the button on my pants, then his own, then took both our lengths in his hand. I thrust into his fist, along his flesh. I braced myself with one hand on the shed and unabashedly moved against him, blinding heat coiling in my groin, wiping all sense from my brain. He dropped his hand off my neck and began lifting my shirt off. I arched back to give him room and a ripping pain went through my torso.

Armise stilled when I flinched. "You are bleeding, Merq."

I stepped back and pulled my shirt completely off, tossing it to the side. The pain was immediate, my body protesting the movement. "What the fuck?" I said as I looked down at the seeping wound, a half-moon crescent slash that ran from just below my left nipple to the bottom of my ribs. The cut was shallow but pulled farther apart with each movement.

When I looked to Armise his brow was creased in concentration. Or frustration? I couldn't read him, couldn't figure out why the minor wound had flipped his emotions so quickly.

He grasped me by the shoulders and put my back to the shed, his fingers gingerly pressing around the cut. "He went for your heart," Armise gritted out. He put his palm to my chest and breathed deeply, steadily, as if he was counting each beat, ensuring that my heart was still working.

"I'm okay."

His head snapped up. His jaw flexed, his eyes narrowed. And still his hand remained over my heart.

"Just fucking touch me," I said quietly, even as my heartbeat thundered in my ears.

His fingers went to my nipple ring, tugged at it, the uncomfortable pull creating sparks of silver in my vision, the ache running through my body in waves. He dipped his head and took my nipple between his teeth, playing with the ring as he licked at the bud. He ran his hands down my torso, over my abs, then he curled his fingers into the hair at my groin, tugging it.

I winced, but couldn't resist the urge to pull a fraction away and amp up the pressure. It sent shockwaves through my body and I couldn't hold back—I needed more.

I grabbed Armise's hand and moved it lower, wrapping his fingers around my balls and tugging gently. Armise reached his fingers back, teasing at my hole. He slid his other hand down to my cock, pumping me with a firm grip. He kissed me with a force I knew would be bruising, leaving my lips swollen.

And still I needed more.

Fuck.

Just more.

That unfamiliar, unnamed feeling began to build back up in me, as if it was competing for my attention, trying to coax me into places my head wasn't willing to go even if my body was.

Before I could think, I was cupping my hand over Armise's and pushing his finger inside me. I bit at my lip, the sudden uncomfortable burn bringing every nerve in me sparking to life.

"Fuck me with your hand," I ordered, pushing him deeper.

A near growl came from Armise, then he was pushing me to the ground, ripping my boots and my pants off and discarding them to the side. He settled between my open thighs and didn't say a word as he pulled his canister of balm from his medkit and dipped his fingers into it. And before I could even think of changing my mind—realizing that he'd only done this to me once before—he had two fingers pushing into my ass.

"Fuck, that hurts," I ground out through clenched teeth.

"Don't fuck with me, Merq. You get off on the pain. Just take it. Just let me"—he dragged his fingers over my prostate, making me arch into his touch—"make you come."

The rocks on the ground jabbed into my back. I could detect the edges of my fresh tattoo because, unlike the rest of my skin, the sensation on that part of my back was dulled nerves and the itch of healing. The scent of Armise's balm and his familiar musk surrounded me, driving the metallic bite of the Committee member's blood from my nose.

I dug my heels into the dirt and pushed back on his hand. The pain speared through me and his cold fingers intensified the nerve-fraying effect. I clamped my eyes shut and rode the movement of his hand as he spread me open, that undeniable emotion clawing at me now, a clamor in my head of memories, of Armise's body under mine, of my tongue on his sweat-slick skin, of my cock driving hard and fast into his ass until all thought except him was wiped away.

This claiming wasn't enough. I needed—I wanted, fuck, so desperately wanted—more than this.

I opened my eyes and spoke before I had time to stop myself.

"Fuck me, Armise."

Armise's gaze became predatory in a split second. He moved his fingers harshly inside me, forcing my body to open to him.

This was uncharted territory for us. I'd never allowed Armise to fuck me, and only one other man ever had. I'd rarely trusted anyone enough to allow them to control me like that. But at that moment I wanted Armise to possess me completely.

I wanted to fucking let go for once. To have control ripped away from me.

To feel what Armise felt when I took him.

His fingers were gone for only a breath then his cock was pushing inside and I felt like I was being torn in half. The sensation was overpowering—too full, too harsh, too foreign—but I gripped his hips and drove him deeper. I accepted the pain that rent through me and let all control go. The agony melding with pleasure, morphing, roaring through my blood, making my hearing fuzz out until all I could do was hold on as Armise pounded into me.

He lifted my hips, setting my legs over his thighs, his thumbs and fingers digging into my flesh. Each pressure point felt like an ice-cold brand on my skin. He wrapped his hand around my cock. The balm still coated his fingers, and the easy slide of his fingers over my dick was gentle in comparison to the harshness with which he fucked me. It made my head spin and I had to clamp my eyes shut to keep from coming right then.

But I couldn't block it all out. Armise was everywhere—his body coiled around me, his hands bruising my flesh, his cock driving deeper inside me with each thrust. His moans filled my ears, ricocheted through my brain, shredding all restraint, imploding my barriers like the blast of a sonicbullet.

I panted, begged, knew I sounded as desperate as I felt. And that just made him take me with more force.

I didn't know how much more I could take. This was torture and desire and fear and lust and I wanted to scream for more, but I didn't know what else he could possibly give me.

My release slammed through me without warning, with a cry ripped from me that made my throat raw from the intensity. I saw stars behind my eyelids, a whitewash of brightness, and I could feel Armise's eyes on me even if I couldn't see them. Even if I couldn't find the will to look at him as he took me apart.

I barely registered the stuttering of Armise's hips, his cock buried to the hilt in my ass, then he collapsed on top of me, his black and silver hair brushing against my chin as he kissed my chest. He rolled to the side with a gruff exhalation.

Armise turned on his side, resting his head on my shoulder. Putting his left hand securely around my hip.

The thought that this was too intimate skittered through my clearing head as I remembered who we were and what we were tasked with accomplishing.

I tried to restrain the urge to curl into his body.

I tried to shut myself down.

I couldn't.

* * * *

We'd known our job would become harder after the first three kills. But we'd had no idea how quickly the remaining Committee members would scatter and disappear. Months passed, countries and continents blending into each other, informants all beginning to look the same, to sound the same—whiny, desperate and cowardly.

As my frustration built, the need for revenge became my only driving force. I'd been able to put the image of

Sarai out of my mind when we were tracking the first three kills. To forget for a time about that stadium and the hundreds of thousands who'd died that night. But now I had too much time to think and too little stimulus.

I obsessed about how to get to Ahriman.

I settled into the darkness of vengeance. Welcomed it. Let it consume me.

And Armise didn't try to convince me to do otherwise.

We were entrenched in the bitter cold of the northern fjords of the UU—the New Year having passed weeks ago—with a half-frozen rain sleeting down on us as we trudged to another informant rendezvous point. This was the first time that Armise was going to make contact with a former co-worker, as it were, since disappearing with me from that stadium.

Manny was a Dark Ops officer for Singapore and Armise insisted that he could be trusted—to a point. I was dubious. But all other avenues of intelligence-gathering had been dead ends.

Armise was hunched over, speaking in low tones to Manny, who was feeding him more intel on the supposed Committee member hiding out in the towering mountains, miles off track and completely off-grid. It was the closest we'd come in months to any of the remaining nine Committee members. The anticipation of ticking another body off our list of kills had me hyped up and ready to move.

My rifle was slung over my chest and I clicked the safety on then off, over and over again, the lever making a mechanical *snick* of metal on metal until Armise whipped his head in my direction. "Fucking stop," he ordered.

Manny's and my breath came out in billows as we exhaled, but the condensation from warmer air meeting the cold was conspicuously absent from Armise. I had no doubt that his skin would match the frigid temps of this northern clime.

I furrowed my brow and set my hands on my hips. He was just as on edge as I was, apparently. Manny's sudden appearance didn't sit right with me. Which was why we'd chosen to meet in the middle of nowhere.

The radio in my pocket crackled as Armise shifted position. Since taking out the last Committee member we'd decided to keep them switched on and in our possession at all times.

I heard a sound off in the distance and cocked my head to get a better read on what it was. Within seconds I knew what was coming at us though, and I yelled for Armise to take cover.

The telltale thump of a Thunder echoed off the steep mountains. The wind whipped wildly around us, driving the rain into my face with icy determination. I skidded to a stop and searched the area, sighting the heli dropping rapidly to the ground in a clearing one hundred feet from where Armise, Manny and I were hunkered down behind the jagged boulders of the mountain.

Even though the side of the Thunder was emblazoned with the orange and yellow sun insignia of the Revolution, I pulled my rifle across my chest then shouldered the weapon, training it on the door in preparation for whoever emerged. Armise did the same, dropping back a step and sliding away from me to cover a different angle.

The rotors of the heli slowed then stopped, and the door opened. I recognized the person immediately despite the winter parka, the tilt of his head as he examined me giving him away.

But I didn't drop my rifle from the firing position even as I stood. "What do you want, Simion?"

"I come all this way to see you and this is how you say hello? Come on, Mig. How about a hug?"

That was when I noticed he was walking with a limp.

I stepped from out behind the boulder. "What happened?"

"Caught in the aftermath of a reverb in the DCR." He pulled up his pant leg, revealing a titanalloy synth. "The doc's got this new kind of surge. Works pretty effectively to mask the phantom pains, but leaves me relatively filterless."

I frowned at his attempt to make a joke. "You're out of commission."

He shrugged. "Reserve, technically. But yeah, I don't think I'm coming back from this. So that's why you're graced with my presence today."

"How did you even find us?"

Manny and Armise emerged from behind their boulder and Simion smiled at Manny.

"It was a generous offer," Manny said with a shrug.

Armise whipped his rifle around and stalked off.

"He'll be back, right?" Simion said.

I watched for a moment as Armise retreated then turned back to Simion, my rifle still shouldered. I didn't care if Manny had been the one to lead us here or that I'd known Simion more years than I hadn't. I couldn't trust anyone right now except Armise.

"Yeah. Now, why are you here?"

"You going to put the gun down? I am disabled."

"Right. You're pretty far away from home and we're supposed to be untrackable. Call it paranoia or instincts, but I'm not putting it down until I know what's going on."

"The president needs you back in the States."

"What the hell is he still doing in the States?"

"The DCR is too unstable. Neveed won't let him go in. He moved to his house on the West Coast for a while, but word got out quickly where he was and the Opposition moved on us. He's back in the bunker now."

"The bunker?"

"The analysts were given intel by the PsychHAgs that is credible enough to make us think an assassination attempt is imminent. I know we can protect him, but Neveed wants more than just reassurances. He wants someone there the president trusts."

"He wants me to come back in."

"Both of you." He gestured to Armise, who was walking back toward the three of us. "Neveed wants to regroup. Talk strategy. We've been notified of three Committee member deaths, but that was months ago."

"It is all we've been able to locate and eliminate," Armise confirmed.

"This takes precedence then. We've got time to get to the others."

I crooked an eyebrow in Armise's direction. He punched Manny in the arm. "You owe me, asshole."

Manny laughed at that. "Will work for cash," he said with a smirk.

We left Manny at the meeting spot and climbed into the massive heli. It took off once all of us were situated for the hours-long flight back to the Continental States.

The Thunder cut swiftly through the clouds and was over the ocean before I knew it. I stared out the window and took in the vastness of the choppy waters as sight of the UU receded. Despite the length of the flight I knew I wouldn't sleep.

I sat back on the creaking, uncomfortable seat of the heli, the beat of the rotors thrumming through my body.

Since neither Armise nor I had comm chips, we were fitted with helmets with internal mics so we could speak to each other over the insistent beat of the Thunder. The heli pilot was someone I didn't know and Simion sat up front with him, leaving Armise and I in the back alone.

I shifted in the seat, trying to find a spot that didn't press against the scar on my back. Even though it had been months since getting the tattoo, it was as if I could still feel it. I'd never been as aware of that wound as I was since getting that mark in Amsterdam.

Armise hadn't asked me about the meaning of the tattoo or why I'd chosen the images that I had. At the time I had gone by instinct, but even I wasn't emotionally bereft enough not to realize the deeper meaning that the mark held for me.

A knife, a bullet, a rope.

All items that could kill. The tools of my survival. Of my success.

But more than that, they were permanent reminders of the events that bound me to Armise in ways I was just starting to admit to myself.

I wasn't ready to speak any of this aloud to Armise. Hell, maybe I never would be. But I knew that what I felt for Armise was unlike what I felt for anyone else in my life.

"Dragged into your darkness again, Merq?" Armise's voice came over the helmet speakers, his accent thick and his tongue twisting over the Mongol dialect he used so that only he and I could understand what was being said.

We'd spoken of darkness before, but my mind had been in a very different place then, even if it was only months ago. His words in the bunker came back to me. *'People need love, Merq. Why else fight?'*

I shook my head, grinned. "No. Pretty far from it, actually."

Armise furrowed his brow and grumbled into the mic, "I will never fully understand you."

I chuckled at the defiant set of his shoulders, and the way he crossed his arms and turned his body away from me, staring out the window. For once, maybe there was a piece within myself that I knew existed, but that Armise couldn't yet see.

Through the clarity of what I could only define as being settled for the first time in my life, the sensation that something was off persisted in me.

I was quite sure we were willingly walking back into hell—the death threat on the president, the remaining Committee members, our search for Ahriman, the rallying of Opposition forces…

But at least I'd have Armise at my side through it all.

I was that bullet. Armise was that knife.

And we were unstoppable as long as we were bound to each other.

Chapter Fourteen

12 September 2558, 2233 hours
Armise Darcan's 38th year
Somewhere in the Atlantic Ocean (not nearly close enough to the United Union)

He did not have to make eye contact with me for me to know. I excused myself from the crew members I had been talking with, stood and followed Merq down the cramped hallway. We were on much quieter waters than we had been for the last week, calm enough that I was not being tossed into the walls every time I took a step. Calm enough that when Merq and I got back to our room he could fuck me against the wall without either of us undergoing too much bodily damage.

I surveyed his form as we made the short walk. There was this curve Merq had in his shoulders when he was stressed, almost as if he was attempting to disappear within himself. It was not so obvious, much more subtle in nature than I was able to convey in thought or words. So much so that it was likely no one else noticed the change in him when it happened. But I did. When

Merq was tense was when he sought me out. I don't think he realized exactly what he was doing. He would pass by me, deliberately taking stock of every other person or item in the room except for me... Those were the times he needed me the most.

Perhaps he did not understand he was seeking me out at all. Call it denial, or an ingrained survival mechanism. Justification, perhaps. I was okay allowing Merq to hide behind the thought that he was never the instigator between us. He did not have to beg to be touched, did not have to ask for permission or state his preferences, I just knew.

He wore his vulnerability like a second skin that pulled taut to protect him—hunched shoulders, balled fists, pronounced frown that could only be kissed away... I seemed to be the only person who could see that layer for what it was. Or perhaps the only person who knew how to remove it.

I pushed down the foreboding building in my stomach, chilling my skin—it wasn't tomorrow yet—and shut the door to our cabin behind me. Merq had his hands on me immediately. His palm pressed into my lower back, fingers scratched at my jaw, at the lack of a beard he was now fascinated with. He mouthed at my neck, sucked my skin between his lips and nipped with his teeth. I arched my head back to give him better access.

I avoided touching his right shoulder—I had since the DCR—because some days a touch there was unpleasant and some days it was painful. But being touched along that long, raised scar was never pleasurable for him. So I hooked my arm under his, cupped my hand around the back of his neck and threaded my fingers through the curling hair at his nape. I set my other palm on his chest and dug my fingers in. He was all muscle, not as solid as I was, but much more agile. Some would have said he incapable of being gentle, but I knew better.

Merq's lips found mine, and I caught his lip piercing between my teeth, tugging insistently on the metal until Merq looked at me. I didn't say anything. There was nothing I could say with words that would draw an honest answer out of him. Once his brown eyes were settled on me—narrowed, questioning, annoyed—I released his piercing.

He had been in contact with someone who had upset him, that much I could see. I would find a way to make discreet inquiries to the crew on whether it had been an external or internal argument. Neither was acceptable, but internal strife was much easier for me to deal with. For me to eliminate. I had grunted my displeasure out loud before I had the presence of mind to contain it, and Merq's features softened with my gruffness.

He licked his lips, chapped from exposure to salt, wind and cold. His bottom lip was fuller than the top, and I loved to suck on it, not just because of the piercing. Because of the way he moaned when I took his lips between mine. Sometimes his responding groan was more intense than when I took his cock into my mouth.

I ran my fingers through his hair, pushing back the strands that were longer than I'd ever seen them. It did not quite cover his eyes yet, but it was getting close. Merq tugged at the edges of my T-shirt, urging me to lift my arms. I reluctantly let him go as he removed my shirt, but I was doing the same to him a second later. Although he had no tattoos, his skin was not unmarked. There was a patchwork of scars across his chest, stomach, ribs and back. The ridges along his shoulder and his neck were the reddest, the angriest despite the number of years since their violation. Merq's torso was covered in battle wounds like my neck and face were.

As if I led with my head and he led with his heart.

I licked around his nipple, bit at it until Merq was clutching at me as if I would disappear. Not needing to go on deck today, I was without shoes, while Merq wore his uniform boots. Which put us at almost the same height. I ran my tongue up the side of his neck, across the jagged scar I'd given him that he'd barely survived… I stopped then, breathed him in, and placed a kiss at the spot below his earlobe where I could hear his ragged breath in my ear. I ran my finger down the line of the five piercings on the shell of his ear, hoops that I knew the origins of even if he didn't think I did. I tugged at the first one and bit at his neck.

Merq forced me back against the wall where we would both have more leverage. Our individual beds were too small to contain one of us fully, let alone two. So the wall became our default surface to work off. I undid the clasp on my pants, undid his as well, and gripped his hips, grinding us together. There were too many layers between us, including Merq's silence about whatever had just happened. We did not speak about it, we did not speak about anything.

I let it all go. He had his secrets, I had mine. But this… I slipped my fingers under his waistband and dropped his pants to the ground. He shivered and smashed his lips against mine. His tongue snaked inside my mouth, searching deep, consuming me and wiping away all thought. Then his hand was on my cock, drawing it into a firm grip with his own dick, and I couldn't remember when he'd undressed me, but this was exactly what I needed.

All I could think about was this second—how much I needed, wanted, had to have him. All I could taste was this second—the mint on his tongue from the drops he used to combat seasickness. All I could hear was this exact second—his breath becoming shallow, ragged, as his dick slid against mine.

Then Merq was dropping to his knees, licking a stripe up my cock as I fisted my hands in his hair. He mouthed at my balls, licking around the sack, then drawing one into the heat of his mouth. And fuck, his mouth was like fire, his tongue like the flash of a brand. Because my skin was so cold it was if his was fevered, and the contrast between us made it feel as if I was going to self-combust.

His tongue snaked back to that smooth patch of skin behind my balls. Merq lifted my leg, draped it over his shoulder and angled me so his tongue could reach all the way back and sweep over my hole. I slammed my head against the wall of the cabin and tried to keep myself upright, there was nothing else I had the power to do.

Merq was relentless in his assault with his tongue, until I was panting, close to actually begging out loud, when he finally added two fingers and thrust them harshly inside me. My body arched into the invasion, pushed down so he could go deeper. His mouth moved from my balls to the head of my cock, to sliding his teeth up the length of me and eliciting a full body shiver I couldn't control.

I pushed him to the floor and turned, straddling his face and dropping my balls onto the vee of his prominent chin. He thrust his fingers into me just as I swallowed his cock to the base, and I knew this wouldn't last much longer. I held myself up with palms planted against the cold metal floor, dropped my head down and buried my nose into his groin. Merq was always clean, meticulously so, but I could smell myself on him, which meant he hadn't showered since getting off by fucking against my hip last night.

Possessiveness stirred within me, a need to protect him, to prove to him that he didn't have to fight me any longer. I ached with the thought of another man's scent on him. As much as I wanted to tear him apart some days, bloody him to the point where I would no longer recognize any of his features that drove me to the point of mad desire, as far as he drove me to the brink of abandoning everything, especially him…

I knew who Merq was. I just had to wait for him to figure it out for himself.

I propped myself up on one hand and ran my other over the insides of his thighs as I took him deep. He bucked into my mouth, his fingers pressing into that spot that had my knees buckling. When his tongue ran up each cheek of my ass then around the edges of my overly sensitive hole, I couldn't hold on anymore. He didn't have to touch my cock at all to get me off. I spilled across his chest, onto his stomach, and seconds later his balls were drawing tight and he was unloading into my mouth. I couldn't swallow it all. I licked his cum from the divot between his cock and his hip then rolled to the floor.

There wasn't enough room on the floor for either of us to stretch out, but neither of us moved. Our quarters were hot and thick with the scent of sex. I breathed it in and attempted to stave off the anxiousness building in my gut now that I'd been ripped away from the present moment.

He hadn't said one word to me during. Or before. Perhaps not today at all, I couldn't recall.

I sat up and draped my arms over my knees, looking down at him. "What happened tonight, Merq?"

He toyed with his eyebrow piercing instead of making eye contact with me. "It doesn't matter."

Except that it did—to me.

He trudged to his feet and into his bunk, falling asleep within seconds. But I couldn't.

I sat on the floor until my neck hurt from my improper posture and my ass ached from the unforgiving surface I had planted it on.

When I looked at the clock set above the door and saw that the time had ticked over to the next day, I knew I would not sleep.

Not today.

* * * *

13 September 2558, 0312 hours

The engine room was the only place on this ship that I could find any peace. Quiet, it was not. The ancient engines roared around me. Only the plugs jammed into my ears kept the rhythmic, deafening clanking from bursting my eardrums. The floor of the room was hot, the air sweltering, laden with engine grease and fuel fumes. It was not peaceful in any way, and yet my sole place to be alone.

I would've preferred to be on the deck, losing all thought to the numbness of cold, but Merq always found me there. And Merq was the last person I wanted to see now that the clock had ticked over to the thirteenth of September.

We'd been on this ship for three weeks, headed for the United Union and our mission to assassinate all of the Opposition members of the Olympic Committee. I had no concern about taking their lives. But regret... The more I considered who I had become, did I regret that the only thing I was good at in this life was death? That was possible.

I was too far removed from my life before the transition. Before a war I'd never heard of stole my family from me. A war—and unforgiving, ruthless men and women—that had tried to tear my soul away from me.

I couldn't stop touching the spot that forever marked this date. My pointer finger was a normal temperature where I circled it around the dimpled flesh remaining from where Merq had taken my fifth digit. But to anyone else, my skin would be ice-cold. A modification that allowed me the luxury of lying on an engine room floor, alone, without dying of heat stroke.

What I considered luxurious should have been laughable, but unlike Merq, I knew that my daily existence could be worse. It had been worse, until the moment twelve years ago that I decided to change my trajectory.

Twelve years ago today Merq had taken my finger.

Twelve years ago today I'd made sure Merq made it out of the DCR alive with the infochip.

For twelve years after that painful date, I'd lived the lie that Merq was my enemy. But perhaps—one month on since Merq had discovered my defection from Singapore—it wasn't as much of a lie as I wanted it to be.

I slapped my hands down on the burning metal floor and pushed myself up, having to use the heel of my left hand to balance as I sat up since my little finger was no longer there. I'd grown accustomed to the accommodations I'd had to make, but I was just as aware of it missing as I had been the day it was sliced from my body.

The loss of that finger should have been inconsequential, I knew that. Yet everything that tied me to Merq was of consequence. There was no way Merq would know what today was, let alone how much of my life had changed this day twelve years ago.

I couldn't find fault in that. Merq's avoidance of the passage or marking of time was one of the things that intrigued me most about him. I, in comparison, grasped on to time as my foundation. It was constant, unchanging. The past was completed—cataloged and accessible—while the future was always one second ahead of me. How I used the second I lived in was completely within my control.

And for today, I would be using every second to restrain myself from pushing Merq off the side of the ship.

* * * *

The engine room door slammed shut behind me and I made my way through the belly of the ship, head ducked to keep from getting a concussion from the low ceiling. I pulled the plugs from my ears, stuffed them in my pocket, and the ship came alive around me. It was the middle of the night, but the crew slept in shifts I couldn't ascertain a pattern to.

"Armise!" a voice called out from behind me.

I gripped the steel beam above my head and turned to see who was calling out for me. The chief engineer was a thin, short man with hands blackened at all times, and his face and clothing covered in gray smudges of grease. He was the smallest man on the ship by far—a stature that allowed him access between mechanical parts. Watching him fix the ship was witnessing feats of dexterity and flexibility I had never seen before. Despite the disparity in our sizes, he wasn't frightened of me.

"Have I not already taken all your money?"

He laughed, then trailed his fingers across his chin, leaving a fresh streak of gray in their wake. "The bursa refreshes my empty pockets tomorrow. Tomorrow. However, I won't speak of wagers today, okay? I have something to show you."

I craned my neck at the grinding sound coming from the engine room. The floor beneath me pitched with sudden movement. "The ship is slowing."

"Yes!" His salt- and time-worn face cracked into a smile. "You must must must come with me."

* * * *

"There was a distress call from one of the States' stations in Greenland," he explained as we walked. "A volcano on their periphery has erupted. Nasty stuff, yeah? Two of our crew have volunteered to go ashore with supplies and assist in the relief. Good boys, they are. They are."

There was the patter of boots on the deck above our heads and the ship pitched to the aft. I cracked my knuckles as I walked a step behind him. "Is it safe?"

"There are few people there as it is, okay? Fewer in port and much more chaos. Neither you nor Merq will be at risk. I promise. I promise."

He was consistently drunk on the overflowing Revolutionary tap. I had no doubt this crew would protect Merq and me with their lives. "I meant the volcano."

He opened the door to the stairs leading to the deck and beckoned me to follow. "There is a storm approaching. Approaching fast. Not a good one, right? The mountains are downwind... I will show you. Come come."

The color of the sky was unlike anything I had ever seen before. To my left it was a shade of orange almost too bright for my eyes. To my right, a dried blood red. And between them a blue pulsation that churned out of the darkness from the distance. My shock must have registered in my face, because the chief engineer pushed a finger into my belly and said, "It's beautiful, innit?"

Beautiful wasn't the word I would have used to describe what I saw in front of me, but one did not quarrel with a man so insistent in his own joy.

"It is," I granted him. "Can I leave the ship?"

"Yes! Of course. Yes. I'll come get you when it is time to take our leave, okay?"

We were being tethered to the dock, the hands of the crew engaged in utilizing rope for something other than binding a prisoner's body into submission. I jumped over the railing and dropped to the dock as soon as we were anchored, the reverberations of my boots echoing against the boat moored next to us.

It had been weeks since I had last stepped foot on solid ground and my body swayed as if anticipating the next rolling wave. The crew dispersed—into the ship or taking off toward the city. There was a spew of lava and a booming thunder that followed on its heels, the spatter of the molten earth falling into the sea not far from the dock.

"Maybe it isn't so safe," the chief engineer called out to me. "Not so safe. I'll let the captain know we need to move soon."

The door leading back into the ship closed and I was alone. Finally.

I stared at the sky, amping up my temp to ward off the biting sleet of rain that began to fall. At least the chaos around me matched my shit mood.

Since we were in Greenland that meant we were a week from the shores of Amsterdam, perhaps a few days more. One more week that I had to find a way to remain on the smallest boat capable of crossing an ocean—without killing Merq. Being in these close quarters with him, for an extended period of time, was chipping away at my patience. I gritted my teeth. I was too patient when it came to Merq.

I slicked my hair off my face with both hands, crossed my arms and closed my eyes. The air here was like Mongolia—bitter cold and dry. Fresh. It had been too long since I had last been home.

I wasn't just years away from the DCR, I was an entire world away. All of that day had been heat—brittle lips, scorching desert, sand-scratched throat—and pain—severed nerves, pulsing blood, joints that ached from my battered body having to carry Merq too far for safety… But here? Perhaps this destruction *was* beautiful, because it was a polar opposite from the DCR—cold and witnessed with a whole, healthy body. But also because I was outside the destruction unfolding before me.

There was a faint click, then the tread of boots on the deck—a footfall pattern of deliberate, practiced and lethal movement that I would recognize in my sleep. I tensed. I hadn't had nearly enough time away from Merq to settle my fraying nerves.

But he didn't approach me.

I maintained my spot on the dock, held my ground, and watched the sky and earth battle in front of me.

Merq remained quiet. That was normal. But there had been a part of me that hoped something would change when he found out what I had given up for him.

He stood at the railing of the deck, looking out over the scene in front of us. Then he settled himself atop the red metal barrier. Streaks of blue lightning glinted off his lip and eyebrow piercing. He kept his attention steadfastly off me.

He didn't think I was watching him, but I was.

Through the corner of my eye I saw him pull a jacket over his shoulders. My jacket—in near pristine condition from disuse. But it wasn't unworn. Even I had needed cover the day we encountered a squall that threatened to capsize the boat, and everyone had worked to clear the deck of hazards and rebalance the ship.

I had spent hours in that coat. Sweating, because I couldn't find an internal temperature setting that balanced the stinging, frigid Atlantic air and the heat that built at my core from slinging cargo all day.

Merq had a coat of his own he had worn that day. But right now, he wore mine.

He brought the jacket to his face to swipe away the beads of rain that fell heavily on us, and his hand lingered, chest expanded, as he inhaled deeply with my jacket pressed to his face. I swiped the rain from my eyes and I mirrored his inhalation—breathing in the air that reminded me of home.

It wasn't simply the air that reminded me of home anymore.

I would recognize my birthday in just over a month. Thirty-nine years on this earth, now older than my parents had been when they were killed. And while he wouldn't know the date, or understand its significance, Merq would be at my side when that day arrived.

This battle of wills with my supposed enemy—this war, in all meanings of the word, between Merq and me—was the reason I had turned traitor to my country twelve years ago. His presence was the only reassurance I had that my fight was worth who I needed to be right now.

He kept the last of my soul from being lost.

Index

Timeline of the Borders War

2058 - Winchester rifle built that will be fired in the opening ceremony
2256 - Last Olympic Games held
2256 - Singapore takes over China after nuclear meltdown and the economy collapses
2258 - Borders War officially starts with Singapore's attempt to take over Australia and Russia
2268 - Merq Grayson (Merq's great-grandfather, six generations back) is born
2308 - Sonicbullet technology is invented by Merq Grayson and his name is officially classified
2348 - Last real bullet fired during the war
2352 - Paper records are purged and transferred to electronic format
2372 – Nationalist underground movement formed
2417 - Targeted electromagnetic pulses, unleashed by the Nationalists, destroy all records
2491 –Wensen Kersch born
2493 - Merq's dad, Lucien Grayson, born

2498 - The existence of one remaining infochip begins as a rumor
2502 – Opposition rises
2503 - Merq's mom, Tallitia Grayson, born
2511 – Ahriman Blanc born
2512 – Revolution formed
2518 – Neveed Niaz born
2519 - Armise Darcan born
2522 – Holly Jegs born
2523 - Merq Grayson born
2524 – Ricor Simion born
2528 - Merq's parents "die" in the attack on the capital that places President Kersch in power, Merq becomes a ward of the Continental States
2538 – Merq joins the Youth Peacemaker training program
2539 - Merq and Neveed start sleeping together
2540 - Neveed becomes Merq's handler
2541 - Merq meets Armise in Bogotá through the eye of the rifle scope
2542 - Merq learns from analysts who Armise is
2545 - Jegs is captured in Singapore, and during her rescue Armise kisses Merq for the first time
2546 – Armise slices Merq neck in the Outposts
2546 – Merq learns about his namesake's house in the Northern Territories
2546 - Armise begins working for the States, and the DCR standoff occurs where Merq acquires the infochip and takes Armise's finger in the process
2546 – Truce called in the Borders War, active combat doesn't stop for another two years
2548 - The Consign Treaty officially ending the Borders War is signed in the United Union, Merq is recruited by Ahriman to be a part of the Opposition, Merq and Armise meet up in Bogotá

2549-2553 – Merq lives in Singapore with Ahriman Blanc as part of his protection detail
2553 - Planning and construction begins for holding the first Olympics in the capital city of the States
2558 - Merq reignites the Borders War when he assassinates the Premiere of Singapore, who is also the leader of the Opposition
2558 – Merq and Armise go on the hunt for members of the Olympic Committee

Characters

Merq Grayson – Peacemaker, colonel, and sniper for the Continental States
Armise Darcan - Dark Ops, officer, and sniper for the People's Republic of Singapore
Wensen Kersch - President of the States and commander of the Revolution
Neveed Niaz – Merq's former handler, General for the States
Ahriman Blanc – Former General for the States, leader of the Opposition
Holly Jegs - Peacemaker for the States, major, member of the President's team
Ricor Simion - Peacemaker for the States, capitan, member of the President's team
Chen Ying - nicknamed "the key," mathematical genius and child prodigy tasked with breaking the encryption on the infochip
Tallitia Grayson - Merq's mother
Lucien Grayson - Merq's father
Exley – member of the jacquerie, contractor for the Revolution
Feliu Casas – doctor for the President of the States and Revolution

Manny – Dark Ops officer for Singapore
Sarai Kersch – Wensen Kersch's wife
Grimshaw Jegs – leader of the Nationalists and Holly Jegs' brother

Glossary

Analyst - soldiers tasked with the study and interpretation of intelligence
Blood tie lock – a lock that is preprogrammed to open only for someone with a certain DNA profile
Borders War - a worldwide war that began in 2246 and continued until 2548 when the treaty was signed, over four hundred million people died in the three hundred years it was waged
Chemsense - chemical weapon designed by Singapore, widely used in the Borders War despite being condemned and outlawed
Comm chip - a communication and information transfer device that is either handheld or implanted in the body, often combined with a transport and tracker chip and implanted in a soldier's wrist (see also "transport chip" and "tracker")
D3 – Peacemaker shorthand for "detail, ditch and decimate"
Dark Ops - special forces for Singapore
Dronebots - unmanned aircraft used for surveillance and attack
Infochip - a microchip rumored to be the only remaining depository of humanity's documented history
Nationalists - people who want the five remaining countries to maintain their superpower status to maintain order

Opposition - a movement started by wealthy individuals who wanted to keep the balance of power in their favor, regardless of the formalized power structure of countries
Peacemakers - soldiers for the States
PsychHAgs - shorthand for Psychological Health Agents, a sector of the military with the responsibility of preparing soldiers for surviving the brutality of war with all of their secrets intact
Revolution - a movement started with the ideal of bringing power back to the citizens and seeking to break up the five countries into districts that are representative of their citizenry
Sonicbullet - sound waves harnessed as ammunition that is able to explode internal organs on impact
Sonicrifle, sonicpistol - weapons created to deliver sonicbullets
Surge - medication that places targeted nanoparticles into the bloodstream to speed healing (also highly addictive)
Synth - synthetic limb
Tracker - a chip that tracks the location of the person carrying it, either on or in their person (see also "comm chip" and "transport chip")
Transport chip - a device that allows a person to use one of the sanctioned molecular transfer hubs scattered across the globe, transport is a painful process as the technology is still in its infancy, transport of any person can be harmful or potentially fatal, so its use is limited (see also "comm chip" and "tracker")

Countries of the world in 2558

Continental States (the States)
Leader: President

Color associated with the country: vermillion and yellow

People's Republic of Singapore (Singapore)
Leader: Premiere
Color associated with the country: cobalt blue and silver

United Union (UU)
Leader: Prime Minister
Color associated with the country: royal purple and black

American Federation (AmFed)
Leader: President
Color associated with the country: emerald green and peacock blue

Dark Continental Republic (DCR)
Leader: President
Color associated with the country: gold amber, white, and earth brown

About the Author

I sleep little, read a lot. Happiest in a foreign country. Twitchy when not mentally in motion. My name is Sam, not Sammy, definitely not Samantha. I'm a pretty dark/cynical/jaded person, but I hide that darkness well behind my obsession(s) for shiny objects. I'm the macabre wrapped in irresistible bubble wrap and a glittery pink bow, I suppose.

S.A. loves to hear from readers. You can find her contact information, website details and author profile page at http://www.pride-publishing.com.

PRIDE
PUBLISHING

Lightning Source UK Ltd.
Milton Keynes UK
UKOW02f2231010916

282018UK00001B/25/P